The Breakdown So Far

# Chapters

Store# 00781 Chapters Square One
189 Rathburn Road West
Mississauga,ON L5B 4C1
Phone: (905) 281-8347
Fax: (905) 281-2260

* Thank you for shopping at Chapters *
Store# 00781 Term# 006 Trans# 118858
Operator 203Ko    08/09/2007 14:35

### iREWARDS SALE
### 43716463

***********************************************

| | |
|---|---|
| HARRY POTTER & THE DEATHLY H | $30.22G |
| 551929764 | |
| Original Price | $45.00 |
| 5 off | $-2.42 |
| Rewards Discount | $-3.36 |
| 20% off Harry Potter | $-9.00 |
| BREAKDOWN SO FAR | $15.29G |
| 889225567 | |
| Original Price | $17.95 |
| 5 off | $-0.96 |
| Rewards Discount | $-1.70 |
| EBKINZ BEAGLE | $14.14GP |
| 6137100836.5 | |
| Original Price | $14.95 |
| off | $-0.81 |
| BKINZ GOLDEN RETRIEVER | $14.14GP |
| 681083945.5 | |
| Original Price | $14.95 |
| off | $-0.81 |

***********************************************

| | | |
|---|---|---|
| Items  4 | | |
| Subtotal: | | $73.79 |
| GST | 6.0% | $4.43 |
| PST | 8.0% | $2.26 |
| Total: | | $80.48 |
| DEBIT CARD | | $80.48 |

***********************************************

Your Total Savings: $19.06
Promotions: $9.00
iREWARDS: $10.06

***********************************************

Store# 00781 Term# 006 Trans# 118858
GST Registration# R897192666

*0078100601188581*

en condition de revente peuvent être échangés ou remboursés par une note de crédit pour la valeur de l'article lors de l'achat. Veuillez noter qu'aucun échange ou remboursement ne sera accepté pour les magazines ou les journaux.

If, for any reason, you purchase an item that is not totally satisfactory, please feel free to return it for refund or exchange within 14 days; we simply ask that the item be returned in store-bought condition and be accompanied by a proof of purchase from any of our stores. Items accompanied by a gift receipt and returned in store-bought condition may be exchanged or refunded onto a credit note for the value of the item at the time of purchase. Please note we cannot provide an exchange or refund of magazines or newspapers.

Si vous n'êtes pas entièrement satisfait d'un de vos achats, n'hésitez pas à le retourner pour un remboursement ou un échange dans un délai de 14 jours. Nous exigeons cependant que l'article soit dans le même état qu'au moment de l'achat et que vous présentiez un reçu provenant d'une de nos librairies. Les articles accompagnés d'un reçu-cadeau et retournés en condition de revente peuvent être échangés ou remboursés par une note de crédit pour la valeur de l'article lors de l'achat. Veuillez noter qu'aucun échange ou remboursement ne sera accepté pour les magazines ou les journaux.

If, for any reason, you purchase an item that is not totally satisfactory, please feel free to return it for refund or exchange within 14 days; we simply ask that the item be returned in store-bought condition and be accompanied by a proof of purchase from any of our stores. Items accompanied by a gift receipt and returned in store-bought condition may be exchanged or refunded onto a credit note for the value of the item at the time of purchase. Please note we cannot provide an exchange or refund of magazines or newspapers.

Si vous n'êtes pas entièrement satisfait d'un de vos achats, n'hésitez pas à le retourner pour un remboursement ou un échange dans un délai de 14 jours. Nous exigeons cependant que l'article soit dans le même état qu'au moment de l'achat et que vous présentiez un reçu provenant d'une de nos librairies. Les articles accompagnés d'un reçu-cadeau et retournés en condition de revente peuvent être échangés ou remboursés par un note de crédit pour la valeur de l'article lors de l'achat. Veuillez noter qu'aucun échange ou remboursement ne sera accepté pour les magazines ou les journaux.

If, for any reason, you purchase an item that is not totally satisfactory, please feel free to return it for refund or exchange within 14 days; we simply ask that the item be returned in store-bought condition and be accompanied by a proof of purchase from any of our stores. Items accompanied by a gift receipt and returned in store-bought condition may be exchanged or refunded onto a credit note for the value of the item the time of purchase. Please note we cannot provide an exchange refund of magazines or newspapers.

# Chapters

Store# 00781 Chapters Square One
189 Rathburn Road West
Mississauga, ON L5B 4C1
Phone: (905) 281-8342
Fax: (905) 281-2260

Thank you for shopping at Chapters
Store# 00781 Term# 006 Trans# 118858

TRANSACTION RECORD
INTERAC DIRECT PAYMENT

Card Number : ************4436
Account : DEBIT CARD
Account Type: CHEQUING
Trans Type : PURCHASE
Amount **$80.48**
Merchant ID : 00176364
Terminal # : 02473593   Operator : 506
Date : 07/08/09   Time : 14:36:38
Auth # : 966048   Bank Ref : 0001110
000 APPROVED-THANK YOU

***** CUSTOMER COPY *****

refund of magazines or newspapers.

Si vous n'êtes pas entièrement satisfait d'un de vos achats, n'hésitez pas à le retourner pour un remboursement ou un échange dans un délai de 14 jours. Nous exigeons cependant que l'article soit dans le même état qu'au moment de l'achat et que vous présentiez un reçu provenant d'une de nos librairies. Les articles accompagnés d'un reçu-cadeau et retournés en condition de revente peuvent être échangés ou remboursés par une note de crédit pour la valeur de l'article lors de l'achat. Veuillez noter qu'aucun échange ou remboursement ne sera accepté pour les magazines ou les journaux.

If, for any reason, you purchase an item that is not totally satisfactory, please feel free to return it for refund or exchange within 14 days; we simply ask that the item be returned in store-bought condition and be accompanied by a proof of purchase from any of our stores. Items accompanied by a gift receipt and returned in store-bought condition may be exchanged or refunded onto a credit note for the value of the item at the time of purchase. Please note we cannot provide an exchange or refund of magazines or newspapers.

Si vous n'êtes pas entièrement satisfait d'un de vos achats, n'hésitez pas à le retourner pour un remboursement ou un échange dans un délai de 14 jours. Nous exigeons cependant que l'article soit dans le même état qu'au moment de l'achat et que vous présentiez un reçu provenant d'une

# The Breakdown So Far

## M.A.C. FARRANT

Talonbooks
Vancouver

Talonbooks

P.O. Box 2076, Vancouver, British Columbia, Canada V6B 3S3
www.talonbooks.com

Typeset in Mrs. Eaves and printed and bound in Canada.

First Printing: 2007

The publisher gratefully acknowledges the financial support of the
Canada Council for the Arts; the Government of Canada through
the Book Publishing Industry Development Program; and the
Province of British Columbia through the British Columbia Arts
Council and the Book Publishing Tax Credit for our publishing
activities.

**Library and Archives Canada Cataloguing in Publication**

Farrant, M. A. C. (Marion Alice Coburn), 1947–
    The breakdown so far / M.A.C. Farrant.

ISBN 978-0-88922-556-5

    I. Title.

PS8561.A76B74 2007      C813'.54      C2006-906486-5

*For Terry*

# Contents

## 3. A TALENT FOR SUBVERSION

## 4. PERPETUAL CODA

*1.*

## Jesus Loves Me
## but He Can't Stand You

# NOW IS THE TIME

The Christian roofer has been phoning us for six years. He has some hope that we will ask him to replace our roof. He phones regularly throughout the year, every two or three months. One year he phoned on New Year's Eve.

"Hello," he said in the slight Eastern European accent we'd become accustomed to. "George, here. Would you be thinking of replacing your roof in the coming year?"

It was 10:30 in the evening. The video had just ended, and we were hanging around the kitchen counting down the minutes to midnight. We'd watched the kettle boil and were sharing a teabag: two cups, one bag. I'd brought out the festive tin of leftover Christmas cookies.

"Not right now," my husband told George. "I'm sorry, but we do not need a new roof."

We're pleasant to George because George is pleasant to us, even if he is persistent. "Did he say 'Happy New Year'?" I asked, somewhat anxiously. It was a lonely New Year's Eve: the two of us, the video, the teabag.

"No," my husband said. "Just that he'd call again in three months. Mark that on the calendar. I'm sure George has. It's something we can all look forward to."

Once George left a message on our answering machine asking us to return his call. Which we did, thinking for some reason he may be ill and that we were the only people he could contact in his time of need. We were disappointed to reach *his* answering machine. The message said, "Hello. George here. Would you be thinking of replacing your roof in the coming year?"

The way we discovered that George was a Christian happened during a call in which my husband, as usual, had turned him down. Then George tried a new tactic, suggesting we call *him* when we'd decided to proceed with a new roof. "But don't call on a Tuesday evening," he told us. "That's Bible study night."

The fact that George was a Christian interested us; we wondered how far his faith in one day replacing our roof would carry him. And because we're not Christians *per se*, trying as we do to dwell contentedly in transience, we wondered what effect his faith might have on us over time. Would he be calling for the next twenty years? Would the three of us grow old together while our roof overgrew with moss and continued to lose shingles in windstorms, while we continued to gently tell him, "No, thank you George. Not this year." Would the presence of George in our lives become as comforting as ritual? Would his phone calls become, in spite of our secular orientation, like a knot in the thick rope of our reasons that was hauling us through the years?

The idea of our contacting him about the roof was short-lived. Before long his quiet, intermittent calls resumed. What is it, we asked each other, that causes George to believe so surely that one day he will replace our roof? And how did we acquire this random person in our lives so that now his calls have become like calls from long-ago friends, both dreaded and strangely desired?

Then after six years this thought occurred and it startled us: The true reason that George is phoning about our roof is that this is his job in life—he is a roofer—and to get jobs he calls people up. He doesn't have a personal relationship with us at all, nor is he calling to facilitate our meditations on the nature of our lives, or even to imbue us with Christian beliefs.

When we thought this thought we felt bad. Bad for having so blithely and self-centeredly missed the obvious. Bad that for six years we may have strung along an honest, hard-working man. A decent person. We felt especially mean to have done this. Further, we felt that such meanness of spirit may have contributed to our succession of lonely New Year's Eves, and to our transient existence being, we had to admit, a state less than fulsome.

So we finally asked George to do something about our roof. After six years my husband called him up—it was a Saturday morning—and said, "Now is the time, George."

George didn't sound surprised or overjoyed to hear from us. He merely stated in his usual calm way that he'd arrive at our house that afternoon between the hours of two and four.

When at last we saw him we felt cheered by his appearance; he was exactly as we'd imagined after six years of telephone calls: small, meek, fair-skinned, about sixty-five years old, wearing beige work clothes and a baseball cap. His truck was new and very clean, as we knew it would be.

He nodded to us as he climbed his aluminum ladder to the roof to look things over. From the driveway below we watched him poking at the shingles, and then take a few moments to gaze at the view. A while later we could hear him whistling "Rock of Ages."

When we asked him how he was getting on he called down, shaking his head sadly. "You'll need a complete roof replacement." He was standing on our roof in quiet triumph and telling us, "It's the moss on the shingles. It's the terrible rot within."

And then we couldn't agree more. For the first time in six years we felt as if a load was about to be lifted. The terrible rot within was about to be removed. It was a bright day in early December with the sun glinting off George's glasses as he began his solemn descent down the ladder. Right there in the driveway, as George drove away with the promise of a new roof before Christmas, we began planning a crowded New Year's Eve party—loud, boozy, sinful.

# OUR EYE IN THE SKY

We decide that Mr. Manager, our eye in the sky, has been sending us hoax messages.

Today's message: Soren Kierkegaard was right.

This throws us.

Meaning what, we ask? That the best course all along has been surrender?

This makes us laugh.

Last week he sent word that the sun is closest to divine panic. We have no problem with this idea—with the necessity of hiding beneath umbrellas.

But Kierkegaard?

We talk it over. Surrender to what? War? Plague? Old age? Fear? God? D ... d ... d ... d ... eath?

It's a joke, says one of us. Mr. Manager's having us on.

It's a plot, says another. Engineered by the Irony Club.

We're the Irony Club, says a third.

Ah.


We replace Mr. Manager with Madame Miner.

Madame Miner pans for revelations. So far—gravel.

But—any day now ...

# NO EXCUSE

They are having a talk with the baby.

You're two and a half years old. It's time you got a job.

The baby wails.

What did it say? asks the father.

Something about having just learned to walk, says the mother.

That's no excuse, says the father. I got my first job at the steel mill when I was nineteen months old.

The baby wails.

What did it say?

Something about not being fully toilet-trained, says the mother.

That's no excuse, says the father. That steel mill job? I shit my pants every day. Three times a day!

Father's right, the mother tells the baby. You've hung around long enough. Time you paid your way.

The baby wails.

What did it say?

It's got a headache, says the mother.

That's no excuse, says the father. Everyone's got a headache. It's what happens when you take your place in the workaday world. I've had a headache since I was nineteen months old!

The baby wails.

Now what?

It says go jump in the creek, says the mother.

My god! cries the father. That's what Uncle Beverley said! It's going to turn out like Uncle Beverley! He didn't leave home till he was eight!

That settles it, the mother tells the baby. You'll start looking for a job this week.

One day you'll thank us, says the father.

The baby wails.

What did it say?

That there's been some terrible mistake, says the mother.

Oh that, says the father. Everyone says that!

What a relief, says the mother. That means the baby's normal.

Thank god, says the father. I was beginning to have my doubts.

## TOO LATE

Once again they are having supper. Father puts down his knife and fork and smoothes an eyebrow with his finger. Then—a low rough sound—Grrrrr ... This is the signal for Mother to rip the dress off Grandma. Mother hates anything old or holey. She laughs her head off, rip by rip. Sister can't stand the fun and jumps up, twirling around the table. Brother makes farting sounds with his mouth like a ventriloquist and soon Uncle joins in. He tilts his head to the ceiling and screams—Caaawww ... Caaawww ... By now the dog is delirious. He climbs onto the table. Of course! His birthday! Everyone sings *Happy Birthday, Dear Buddy* and then Grandma, in her slip and elastic bandages, belches out the first five notes of "Roll out the Barrel."

The neighbours worry about the loose minds next door. They get up a petition. It's not so bad now, say the neighbours. But what happens if their minds get really loose? It's terrifying to think of such derangement running free.

Too late. Grandpa has escaped and carted off the neighbour's baby. He's got the baby on the front lawn and is licking the chocolate crucifix around its neck. The baby is laughing and laughing.

# VALENTINE

A man quotes a Valentine inscription: *Poetry will keep you young. Forget bringing lumbering women to climax. Too soon the body jerks out of reach.*

What do you think? Do you think she'll like it?

His friend at the table says, Nice. Not bad. Or you could use this: *Poetry is an electrically powered stuffed horse with a sign around its neck that says, "Everything Seems Black Today Except the Firmament."*

I don't care for that. Can't get my mind around that.

A third friend says, Then try this. This is good. *We are born astride the grave, the light gleams an instant ...*

Yes, that might motivate her.

It's catchy. It'll get her attention, says the second friend.

Might scare her my way ...

For fuck's sake, says the fourth friend, why don't you try this: *We are all born mad. Some remain so.* Now cut the crap. Deal the frigging cards.

Oh, Sam, says the third man. You're such a rough little wordsmith.

No, I like it, says the first man. It gives a certain comfort ...

Ties things up ...

Exactly.

What about her?

Who?

Her. The valentine. Will she like it?

I don't know. "Mad" is so strong.

Change it to "madcap": *We are all born madcap* ...

There's an idea, says the first man. Promise laughs. She'll come running. And why not? Laughter is a kind of love ...

# INSEPARABLY LINKED

An old woman is writing an ad. Her daughters lie on the motel bed. They're fake Siamese twins, fat, thirty-seven and forty-one years old. They look like a massive two-headed doll with their blonde wigs and shared pink dress.

The old woman pauses and asks her husband, the old man standing at the window picking his teeth with a matchbook cover: How does this sound? *Those Lovely Girls Happy and Vivacious in Their Inseparably Linked Lives Have Perfected Natural Talents Which Make Them One of the Greatest and Most Meritorious Attractions in the World.*

The girls squeal, happy. They love the ad.

Too wordy, says the old man.

His wife snorts. Trust you to take the narrow view, Mr. Edge of the Picture!

You want business, you write a decent ad, says the old man.

While you stand there picking your teeth …

Their daughters start singing falsetto—*I fall to pieces* …

Not now, shouts the old woman. Save it for the Rotary picnic.

Too bad the girls aren't Pascal Pinon, says the old man. That Mexican. Now there was an act. Painted-shut eyes, a nose, a mouth on the huge tumor that was growing out the side of his head. Covered the tumor with strands of horse hair and called his twin Ramon. There was a guy knew how to draw a crowd …

All I want is a few bookings for retirement homes, says the old woman. A couple of fairs.

Well, says the old man, you couldn't draw a dog with that ad.

The girls start singing *My heart is like a red red rose* ...

I said not now!

Shouldn't that be "hearts"? asks the old man.

The old woman goes back to her writing.

Put in a bit about them having one heart between them, says the old man. One heart two brains. That might bring them in ...

Or one brain two hearts, says the old woman. That's more interesting ...

# THE COMPASSIONATE SIDE OF NATURE

For five weeks we watched the video feed of the eagle's nest. A man had placed a video camera above the nest and we along with several million people sat transfixed before computer screens and watched as a nesting pair took turns sitting on two eggs. It was exciting. Soon we would witness the birth. But mysteriously one of the eggs disappeared. It was then explained via newspaper and TV coverage that this often happens with eagles—an egg may be empty. We consoled ourselves: this was raw nature, after all. Then holes were seen in the second egg and we became excited once again—a chick was about to peck its way out of the egg. But it soon became evident that this egg was also empty. There was great sadness among the several million people. But we continued watching to see what might happen next, if anything, and were not disappointed. Three days after the second egg was discarded a new form appeared in the nest—a miniature dachshund wearing a rhinestone collar. We think—and hope—that the dog is a replacement for the failed eggs. You hear about these things, about the compassionate side of nature. For example, mother ducks adopting abandoned kittens, and so on. Perhaps it is the same situation here. The parent eagles at present seem attentive to the dog; they feed it and have in no way harmed it. And they appear mesmerized by the rhinestone collar, staring at it for minutes on end then tapping at it to see what it might be. During sunrise the collar glints spectacularly. But we fear for the dog. What will happen when the eagles decide it's time for it to fly? Will they push it from the nest to its certain death? A rescue operation has been mounted. The world watches as firefighters, who have a well-deserved reputation for rescuing cats from trees, confer with wildlife experts. The great worry is that the eagles will be spooked by human intervention and fly off with the dachshund in a bid to protect it from predators. The dog's name is Bismarck. His owners, an elderly couple who live in a cottage nearby, are receiving trauma counselling. Meanwhile scores of grief workers are on standby should the story end badly.

# HENS

There was something funny by the side of the road. I saw it out the side of my eye as I drove along. It was my two aunts and Grandma returned from the dead. They were clucking together like hens.

Everything was black and white.

A voiceover said, "A family of hens lands by the side of the road and spies a pile of cigarette butts! What will they do?"

It was George Page speaking, for many years the soothing voice of the TV show *Nature*.

By now I'd stopped the car. There was a cloud of ash around my aunts' and Grandma's feet.

George Page said, "The hens are having a bath! In the animal kingdom, scratching, pecking the ground, laying eggs, wing-flapping, and dust-bathing in a pile of cigarette ash are all normal hen behaviours."

It was wonderful to hear George Page's voice again, those warm, round tones that made *Nature* so endearing. And it was good of him to remind me that I am living in the animal kingdom. I often forget that, in the same way that I forget I am on a planet, one of millions in a universe without end.

It was comforting to see my aunts and Grandma. They were so involved with the cigarette ash, slapping it on their aprons, laughing away.

## FAMILY OF FOUR

They're tearing along the highway towards the Glass Castle—a tourist attraction made of embalming fluid bottles—when they see a giant bug painted on a billboard. A balloon coming out of the bug's mouth says, *Don't be a litterbug! Pick up your garbage!*

Would you look at that! screams Mom and throws an empty nachos bag out the window.

The litterbug has a black eye-patch, green wings, a black and yellow striped body like a bee, and is smoking a cigarette. There's a mound of garbage at its feet.

Smoking kills, says Pop, tossing out an empty pop can.

Too true, says Mom. And so does garbage in the car. Know what I'm saying?

Sure do! says Pop. What are we? Slobs?

Not us, says Mom. We don't live in a stinking mess. We're super clean!

*Broad smiles erupt from the family of four ...*

The kids in the back seat are good kids. They do as they're told and gather up their garbage—gum wrappers, chip bags, the grade five report on trees, a hated sweater, cheese sandwiches, used Kleenex. Everything—out the window!

Then they look at Grandma. She's sitting beside them in her straw hat clacking her false teeth. Smelly nutbar Grandma.

She sounds like a horse called Daisy, says one of the kids— Clippety Clop ... The other kid grabs Grandma's teeth and tosses them out the window. Bye-bye horsy.

Grandma pays no notice. She's singing *Four and twenty black-birds baked in a pie.* Stomping her feet to the song.

Mom! We threw Grandma's teeth out the window!

Good for you. Those teeth were driving me crazy.

Maybe now some peace and quiet, says Pop.

That'll be the day, says Mom.

Just then Grandma farts.

*Screams of* Pee Eeeeu! *from the family of four ...*

'Nuff's 'nuff, cries Pop, screeching the car to a halt. That day has arrived!

They shove Grandma onto the side of the road and speed off. Next stop: The Glass Castle.

We'll get her on the way back, says Mom.

Maybe not, says Pop.

*Boisterous laughing from the family of four ...*

Grandma, meanwhile, wanders about in a field littered with fast food cartons, beer cans, torn-apart garbage bags, and abandoned sofas singing *Pease porridge hot, pease porridge cold ...*

There's a pounding sun, wind, dust ...

The litterbug spies her from his billboard and flies down beside her. He's fifteen feet tall but he doesn't scare Grandma.

She looks up past his insect legs to his green wings, his eye-patch, and his kindly face and sings *I'm a little teapot short and stout ...*

That's fine, m'am, says the litterbug who is actually an undercover bug—Constable Bugle. His mission? Combat Elder Dumping, a current terrible scourge. From his perch in the billboard he has seen it all. Now he flies off with Grandma to the rescue care home ...

Next it's Mom, Pop, and the two kids. They're apprehended outside the Glass Castle loaded down with souvenirs from the gift shop.

Constable Bugle dispenses with the interview, snatches them up, flings them into his portable trash compactor, and flips the switch.

*Screams of outrage from the family of four ...*

## SPRING IN NORTH AMERICA

A man sits on a city curb with fir seedlings attached to his hair and a sign that reads: *The Civil War Starts Here.*

A girl called Plain Trouble sits nearby. Her sign reads: *Potent Guys Please Apply.* She wants a baby but most of the sperm is dead.

A boy holding a plastic cup for change joins them. His name is Ozone. His sign reads: *I've Got Early Decadence Syndrome.*

A gang of children passes by and throws hamburger cartons at them. Otherwise—anonymity.

It is spring in North America. The sun shines in biblical slants through the buildings. Light glints off windows, chrome, sunglasses ...

A crew across the street has set up a sign that says *Filming in Progress.* They're working on a popular TV show called *Final Decisions.* Today's segment follows a woman while she purchases a dress for an important End Times Banquet. To spice things up the producers will add a vicious white monkey who is infected with the Ebola virus. After the dress is purchased the monkey will chase the woman through city streets.

A crowd gathers to watch the shoot. Many hold placards with the shopping woman's name writ in large letters. Beneath her name: *We Love You.*

A derelict couple pauses beside the three on the curb. They're worn out from wandering and sit down. The woman carries a sign that reads: *Who Would Have Dreamed?* The man: *Poems by Bob Buddhism.*

Since it is spring in North America, there's warmth on faces, hands; a gentle breeze blowing cartons along the pavement ...

# TOUR

A woman has a business driving tour busses through an old people's quarter. The tour is mandatory for all persons reaching the age of forty-five.

The bus is clean, air-conditioned; the seats are upholstered and every seat is always filled. It passes through a ten-mile strip of shopping malls before turning into a maze of side streets. Here old people are housed in crowded trailers.

The tour guide speaks to her passengers through a headset. Her voice is stern, matter-of-fact. When she's not speaking, a subdued version of Beethoven's Fifth kicks in.

She points out the sights. This man here, she says, indicating a man staring out a window, once wrote a seven-hundred-and-fifty-page book. And this woman, the one sitting backwards in her rocker, once had a life filled with children and love. This one, she says, indicating a tiny woman in a wheelchair, was called The Woman Who Spreads Her Legs. On motel beds, standing before fireplaces, any time attention was given. In her day she made it a point to select complicated video games for her children so she'd be free of them for a while. The children attacking the games like professional technicians. Where are they now? Never forget, she tells her passengers. This is what some of us come to ...

Not every passenger takes pictures. Some record their impressions on hand-held recorders; some give running commentary on their cells; some wear sunglasses and refuse a window seat; some drop acid and attempt to describe their visions; some take refuge in sleeping pills; some hide small dogs in their jackets though this is not allowed; some sit wide-eyed in the front rows; some lie drunk in the back ...

During my tour I cracked quotes to the comatose. I said, "On the bottom of the sky is a man standing on earth, flapping his arms." I said, "Seven billion years before my birth I was an Iris." I said, "You're all assholes—god love ya!"

# REPORT TO CROWN AND ANCHOR INSURANCE

I spilt tea on the new tablecloth. A tablecloth from France, blue and yellow, very chic. I'd bought it half-price, a bargain. I'd had it seven weeks. A full cup of tea staining the centre of the cloth. I rinsed it under cold water then hung it outside to dry. It was a beautiful day; the sun was shining. Later I drove to town; the Stones were playing loud on the car radio— "Sympathy for the Devil." I felt good. There'd be no crying over spilt tea today. Then things went wrong at the bank. I was overdrawn $257.63. I run a tight ship and was shocked. But I'd forgotten four outstanding cheques. I transferred money, then withdrew some cash for groceries and went shopping. Afterwards there was a hailstorm. Driving home, splats of hail as large as quarters hit the windshield. Briefly, I admired the sky, which was black along the horizon, dark grey above. I sneezed and became aware that my throat felt raw. I worried about getting sick. Reaching home, it was still hailing. I unloaded the groceries and got wet. I suppose the job could have waited until after the storm, but that's another fault of mine. Besides being forgetful about cheques, I must complete each task fully. It's Zen. Years ago I read that this is the way things must be done. I have never forgotten it. It struck me then as an unyielding law of nature, something best not to tamper with. One thing at a time. It could be my motto. Since I was already wet, I decided to check the clothesline: the tablecloth was soaked through. I wrung it out and put it in the dryer. A brief thought crossed my mind: cotton will shrink in the dryer. I ignored the thought. Enough to think about with changing my wet clothes, with putting the groceries away.

With a cold coming on. And hailstones smashing the wisteria above the front porch; the blooms were slippery mauve on the walkway. Feeling chilled, I lit the papers and milk cartons that were stuffed inside the fireplace. They went up with a roar. Soon after I smelled smoke and this made me feel warm. I counted the tins of cat food because once the checkout girl had forgotten to put all the tins in the bag, and I like to plan the cats' meals a week in advance. The cans were all there. Tonight: Seafood Supreme. The phone rang. My neighbour across the street. "There's a lot of smoke coming out of your chimney." I went outside and saw flames. The hailstorm had stopped as if it was a lie, had never happened. The sun was blazing; there wasn't a cloud; the wisteria blooms were dry on the walkway; it looked as if we'd just had a wedding. My roof was on fire. I called 911. They were a long time coming because the fire trucks were at the high school. Someone had thrown a fire bomb into the principal's office. Half my roof burned before the fire trucks got here. Half the school burned down, as well.

# TURNING INTO POPEYE

I worry about turning into a female Popeye—the thinning hair, the shrinking body, the fact that spinach no longer carries the same punch ...

When I have this thought my father visits. Dead for twenty-five years, he's wearing a long black shirt. We go for a swim—something we never did together in life—and his shirt floats about him like an oil spill. We swim in a chlorinated pool, not the ocean, because my father hates the ocean. He'd spent his life on ships in the Pacific. "If I never see another wave I'll be happy." He said this often during his later years.

Swimming beside him now I am shocked by his appearance; he's bald and puny, even with the shirt. I didn't think it was possible for a daughter to become exactly like her father but I am convinced he's returned to tell me the worst: I will turn into a female Popeye as I had feared; I will become a bald and puny old woman wearing black.

My next thoughts are of chin hairs, and squinty eyes, and how I'd rather be Olive Oyl with her flabbergasted cackle. Or even Brutus. Being whacked all the way to the moon doesn't seem so bad anymore.

My father interrupts these thoughts, too. "Bald? Puny?" he says. "So what? Listen, I'll give you a tip."

He then explains the Theory of Combustible Imaginations, something he says he's just dreamed up. "It's about sparks igniting," he tells me. "How fired-up imaginations can ignite other imaginations from a kick-start to a sustained state of charged and delighted thinking ... "

"And?"

"Learn to practise this theory."

"And?"

"It's more satisfying than fear."

# FRIDGE MAGNET PEOPLE

On the plane to Toronto I sat beside a man who was touring cross-country with fridge magnets. "I've got the latest thing in fridge magnets," he said, snapping open his case. "They're called Types." He showed me his samples—miniature people that lit up when stuck to a smooth surface. There was a woman jogger in a blue track suit; a bank manager with a menacing look on his face holding a sheaf of documents; a kid in a backwards ball cap balanced on a skateboard; an old woman in a fur coat with a look of pride on her face. The salesman was doing five home shows in two weeks.

I started seeing fridge magnet people everywhere. For example—myself. I was a woman in black clutching a book, the latest thing in imagination this season. I was on a book tour—one city in half a day. I lit up when stuck to a podium.

The stewardess lit up when her hands made contact with the tray while serving our drinks. She told us she was going on tour next week with a cookbook for people with gluten intolerance. There'd be TV interviews throughout the province of Ontario.

In the hotel café the waitress lit up while cleaning the counter and telling me about her sulfur-crested cockatoos. She'd be touring with them in summer—four bird shows in three weeks.

When I returned home my husband—middle-aged, jeans, grey beard—lit up when his hand slapped his forehead; he'd had a brain wave. "Why haven't I thought of this before?" he said. "Smith!" nodding at our nineteen-year-old cat. "I'll organize a motivational tour. Smith's story can provide inspiration to elderly cats and their owners." The cat lit up when stuck to my husband's lap.

At the Dollar Store the gum-chewing teenager with the eyebrow ring lit up while working the shiny keys of the cash register. She told me she was going on tour with her dad. "He's filming the faceless," she said. "There aren't that many faceless people left. He's found one old guy hiding out in a shed in Saskatchewan. It's that guy's boring story. Boring's the new cool."

Alighting on smooth surfaces—it seemed some kind of key ...

## MESSAGE FROM THE MILKMAN

Since the milkman handles your account we will not be calling upon you to speak before the Assembly. If the Assembly was once interested in what you had to say, this is no longer the case. Your petition for a new mindset has been declined. The Assembly has decided that Loafing, your brand of illuminated living, as you call it—of Buddhist-envy married to brash Western temperaments—is not a feasible mindset for the twenty-first century. The twenty-first century will be dominated, like all the other centuries, by a mindset of doom.

Furthermore, the milkman has filed his report and it is not favourable. You have been pink-slipped as a cultural entrepreneur. The milkman knows all your vices and your needs and will be able to give us an up-to-the-minute accounting of your condition on your behalf. Not that it will be of any help to you. As far as the Assembly is concerned you are a shut book. Do not consider an appeal. Your personal example of illuminated living has tipped the scales against you.

The milkman believes he understands your condition better than anyone and is naturally concerned at your declining milk consumption. He is also concerned about the pile of vomit that has been appearing on your doorstep each and every morning of late. He fails to understand the message contained therein. About the quarrelsome bull tethered to the side of your house, the milkman has lost all patience.

## MEMBERSHIP DRIVE

Two members of the Ponderers Club are put in charge of promotion. Membership has been declining. They hold a press conference to kick off their campaign.

There's a popular misconception that pondering is limited to certain kinds of persons, the woman explains from the podium to the one reporter who shows up. Sad sacks, party poopers, doomsters, depressives. This is just not so. Pondering crosses all demographics. Anyone can ponder!

That's right, says the man. Given half a chance pondering could become your basic Everyman condition.

The reporter asks, What? You mean deep thinking?

You could call it that, says the man. But it's much more. It's about experiencing pits of confusion and dread very deeply, and also boring to the core of everything, analyzing meanings and reasons. Laughter, for example. Or transience. Now there's a killer.

Careful, Stan, says the woman. You don't want to scare people off. What Stan means, she says to the reporter, is that ponderers weigh and think things over. "Everything in Ponderation." That's our motto.

Very good, Gwen, says Stan. But what I was trying to say is that ponderers are anti-surface.

No need to get huffy, Stan, I was only ...

Then please ...

What we're trying to get across here, Gwen says to the reporter, is that there's more to pondering than meets the eye. Pondering can be a fun activity.

Putting a bit of a light spin on things, Stan says, aren't you, Gwen?

The reporter interrupts: But deep thinking. I can't see it. In my pocket of actuality there's the man seeking revenge and the wounded man lying in a hospital bed, and there is constant gunfire but no resolution. What of this?

We live in ponderous times, says Stan.

Okay, but what of the damaged?

Ah, the damaged, says Gwen. This is a music we ponderers know. Also traffic, the tarot, our sacred streets, men in white crying for salvation, clouds. What else?

Ponderance, Gwen, says Stan. We know about ponderance. Which is our mission statement here.

What Stan means, says Gwen, is that we need to keep things on track.

Finally, says Stan.

But deep thinking, says the reporter. I once knew a guy who had his head up his ass. All the time. You mean like that? Doesn't seem like a fun thing to me.

Well, said Stan, we'd have to look at what fun really is ...

Careful, Stan. There's a preponderance of guys not ready to be outed.

My point exactly, Gwen. Which is why we've got to keep things general. Think of Martin and Gary and Brad and Imelda. They may be extreme ponderers but they deserve our respect like anyone else.

Are you suggesting I don't respect extreme ponderers? says Gwen.

I'm not suggesting anything, says Stan. I do wish you'd shut up.

Another guy, says the reporter, kept his nose in his armpit. Eventually his brains leaked onto the floor. I don't call that a fun thing either.

Of all the nerve, says Gwen.

## JESUS LOVES ME BUT HE CAN'T STAND YOU

I'm drinking alone this Christmas.
I've hired a wino to decorate my home.
I've put a bar in the back of my car so I can drive myself to drink.
Jesus, will you be drinking with me this Christmas?
Will you be thinking of me if you do?
My head hurts and my feet stink.
I don't know whether to kill myself or go bowling.

---

*Compiled from C&W song titles.*

# 2.

# Poof

## THERE WAS A FORKLIFT

There was a forklift operating out of the sky depositing singular visions.

There was a bird playing bingo in an attempt at words. Under the "I" was hour.

There was a box of wind undermining egos—poems with shattering views.

There was a group of prancing literary friends sharing ironic discovery.

There was a suspended girl dangling over the parade who'd been put in charge of promotion.

There was a travelling saleswoman whose product was words—hers was a quest of honour.

There was a bird of prey decked out in leather reading a poem about light.

Still—they turned off the light. Perhaps, in dreaming, something new ...

# MICKEY

The liver transplant from cat to cat was a success. Not so successful was the birth of the baby who looked initially like a white mouse. He grew so rapidly they called him Mickey, after the celebrity.

Mickey was wily and changed shape often, from mouse to pig, and back again. But they suspected—the mother and her girlfriend—that the baby was doomed. First, because the mother had done everything wrong including drinking and smoking during pregnancy which, of course, was quick, maybe fourteen weeks. And second, because the father was from a sperm bank in Alberta.

They wondered now how reputable the sperm bank company was.

They wondered if there'd been a mix-up with the vials.

Yet they quickly grew to love Mickey and became devoted to him. Each morning was a surprise and a delight to them because they never knew what form they'd find him in. Usually it was the mouse or the pig, but once it was a beautiful black panther the size of a football. All day the panther lay on the mother's lap and purred.

When Mickey got a little older, the girlfriend, for fun, would chase Mickey beneath the summer house. She loved the way he sounded like a huge mouse scrambling beneath the floorboards. Then she'd entice him out with a block of cheese.

Now and then they'd set Mickey on a board game filled with treats. It was absorbing to watch which treat he would nibble at first. The chocolate truck? The crust of bread? The three slices of bacon?

But at eight months Mickey became ill. The mother was bereft; the girlfriend sobbed; the sperm bank company sent an email of regret.

During his last hours they marvelled still as Mickey rapidly changed form—from pig to mouse, and back again. The change always began with the feet—claws dropping off, fur changing to hide—and progressed upwards to the head.

"Perhaps he keeps changing form so fast," the girlfriend mused, "because he can't settle on a single form and this is what's doing him in. This is what's doomed him."

"Doom," the mother wailed. "How much longer will doomed creatures continue to steal our hearts?"

# BECAUSE OF RUSSELL EDSON

They are clearing out old theories, their no-longer-fruitful theories: the theory of possible; the theory of want; the theory of restlessness; the theory of wandering; the theory of lizards; the theory of coffee mugs; the theory of figure skating lessons; the theory of clocks.

They've shoved the old theories into garbage bags and set the bags at the end of the driveway. A propped sign says *Free*.

Behind the living room curtain they watch who stops by.

A boy on a bike takes the theory of lizards.

Predictable, says the son.

A woman with a dog drags off the theory of clocks.

She's old, says the mother.

A woman pushing a stroller grabs the theory of want.

Makes sense, says the father.

The daughter lets out a scream. You threw out the theory of want? While I was still using it?

We thought, says the father.

How could you? It goes with the theory of desire!

We got rid of desire last summer, says the father.

You what? screams the daughter.

Oh dear, says the mother.

We've still got the theory of open, says the son.

Open? shouts the daughter. That old thing? I wouldn't be caught dead.

Dead? says the father. We threw out dead when you were born.

Oh dear, says the mother.

Now I'll never, cries the daughter.

Never? says the father.

Shut up! screams the daughter.

Didn't we give never to your cousin Shirley? says the mother.

Shut up! Shut up!

## THE WOMEN WITH NO LEGS

Someone has cut off an old woman's legs and it wasn't a man.
It was another legless old woman, one of many who live like rats
in the basements of department stores. They're a dangerous
group, always on the prowl for recruits and replacement legs.
They pull themselves along on their elbows. Once, when they
had legs, they were agile and hopped like monkeys onto
dinner tables to serve the family meal. Or scurried up flights
of stairs carrying baskets full of children, amazing everyone.
Now their hacked off stumps are feared. And the sight of their
hair which is worn entwined with snakes and wreaths of blood.
No one wants to join their party, but you can't avoid them.
Each day they commandeer the public airwaves and broadcast
their savage music, a discordant clashing of cymbals, horns,
accordions, and drums. This means one or more of them has
become a legless corpse and the hunt for replacements is on.
We put on our steel pants then, wait for the all clear ...

## SIXTY DEGREES

The first thing our friend talked about was vampires. He was staying overnight at our house and, while we were having tea, he said there was a woman vampire who lived in his building; she was a regular user of the building's swimming pool. This was in Toronto. He knew she was a vampire because she'd told him so. He believed her. Something about her eyes, the way she stared at him while he swam. Apparently she's from Transylvania, he said, which was a dead giveaway. Ha, ha, he said, dead giveaway. Further, this woman was ugly-looking, with dried, yellowed skin like parchment, and stiff, black hair. Not necessarily vampire-describing qualities, he admitted, and said he only mentioned her looks because they contributed to the menace she exuded. She was about forty-five years old. He, on the other hand, was several years older, a celebrated poet and an artist, a man we admired because he lived, we believed, in a permanent state of wonder. He told us that the vampire followed him into the building's sauna, sat close to him, and pinched his knee. He said he'd never been accosted by a vampire before, and that the incident had scared him. *Freaked* him, was the word he used. He ran from the sauna. This happened during the day and we asked why a vampire was on the loose during the day; we thought they did their evil work at night. Special powers, he said, maybe it's different for the women ones, and maybe they have different rules. A few days later, while he swam lengths—again in the daytime—he told us the vampire swam across the pool and slammed into the side of his body. On purpose, leaving a bruise. This vampire assault was the reason, he believed, that his left eye had later gone funny and filled up with blood. Soon after the vampire disappeared, left the building. Gone on a trip, he supposed, back to Transylvania. The doctor said his eye problem was curious and ordered tests. Meanwhile he'd formed a swimming pool committee. This had to do with the temperature of the swimming pool water, and was not exclusively about the vampire, although she had been involved. There were some residents who liked the water warm, he told us, and some who liked the water cold. The cold water lovers, he said, were dominating the pool temperature. A quiet battle had ensued, which included the bribery of the building manager for access to the pool's thermostat. The cold water lovers, he said, were more affluent than the warm water lovers; they could afford the bribery fees. Because of this they were winning the war. The warm water lovers were mainly a group of frail pensioners, students, and people handicapped in some way, like him with the vampire bruise and the bloody eye, and, as usual, this group was being marginalized and trod upon by those with money. Sixty degrees. That was the temperature they were battling over. The cold water lovers preferred sixty degrees; the warm water lovers, seventy to eighty. Naturally, he said, the woman vampire, when she was in residence, had been among the cold water lovers, no doubt campaigning for an even colder temperature than sixty degrees. Somewhere around freezing, he imagined. Meanwhile, he was waiting for the test results about his injured eye. It was no longer filled with blood but it was sore, and his vision had become impaired. When he left for the West Coast there had been no resolution about the water temperature, nor had he received the test results. But he was glad to leave the vampire behind. At least he thought he'd left the vampire behind. Did we think he had? Yes, we did. Did we think she might find out where he was now living and follow him to the coast? No, we didn't think she would. That's good, he said, she's probably on a vampire vacation; it's spring in Transylvania; she's sure to stay there for the summer. Or maybe she's attending a vampire convention, or a vampire reunion. Or, ha, ha, he said, a vampire festival where hundreds of vampires gather to have workshops and panels and suck each other's blood and talk with agents about selling the film rights to their books. He then mentioned the movie versions about vampires that he loved, the old black and white ones made in the forties and fifties, especially *Son of Dracula*. He liked the Bram Stoker versions, too, and the new movie just out, *Van Helsing*, which, he said, was doing well at the box office. He checked the movie grosses on his computer every night, he said, the daily takes for all the movies playing in theatres across North America, and in the rest of the world. He didn't ask to use our computer that night, though; he only asked for something to eat because he'd missed dinner on the ferry ride over. We gave him a late meal of chickpea soup left over from our dinner, and toast and cheese, and a plate of sweet mixed pickles. He'd missed dinner, he explained, because on the ferry he'd been sitting beside an old woman who had a walker parked in front of her, and they'd struck up a conversation. The old woman was worried about how she was going to get off the ferry when it docked. Where was the exit for foot passengers? He said he'd find out for her because he too was a foot passenger and this was important information. The ferry employee told him: See that wall? The one close to where you're sitting? Well, when the ferry docks, a door opens in that wall, and then you walk through it. He reported back to the old woman: When the ferry docks, you walk through that wall; the wall becomes a door. The old woman became agitated. I'm not walking through any wall, she told him. I'll help you, he offered. No thank you, she said, I'll wait here until my family comes and gets me. When the ferry docked he said it was like magic. Suddenly a door appeared in the wall, and everyone walked through it. The old woman stayed seated and refused to move. When he left her, two ferry employees were trying to convince her to walk through the wall but she wouldn't budge.

He, on the other hand, was not afraid. He walked through the wall with the other passengers, down the steel mesh ramp that showed sea water sparkling far below, and reached the waiting room at the terminal. It was wonderful, he said, walking along with the disembarking passengers. Like being safe in the middle of a herd of humans where no marauding predator could pick you off. Wouldn't it be wonderful, he asked, to be all the time moving through your life like that? It made him think of *National Geographic* specials on TV, the shows about herds of running gazelles and stalking lions. Only the straying young or the infirm were slaughtered. It made him think, once again, about the woman vampire. You don't think she's singled me out for some reason do you? You don't think she'll bother me again? I'm not very gazelle-like. No, we said, it's likely she's someone who thinks she's a vampire but is actually a disturbed person with many problems of her own. Oh, he said, that's a relief. Are you sure? Yes, we said, absolutely. We didn't know if he believed us; though we were certain that an excellent poem or painting would result from his experience.

# OBEDIENCE SCHOOL

They have taken their vacuum cleaner to obedience school. It tears around the house at night chasing the dog, keeping them awake.

And the carpets! cries the woman. It wouldn't know a carpet if you put a gun to its motor!

I fear for the dog, says the man. Whoever heard of a vicious vacuum cleaner?

The man flips a coin to see who'll be the handler. He wins.

Better you than me, says the woman. It's got so I can barely steer it.

Theirs is a pedigree vacuum. It came with a feature called Swivel Glide Vision and headlights so it can see under the bed.

For the first class at the school gym they take along the required equipment—an extension cord and a hammer. But can't get beyond the door. A crowd of rowdy vacuums has downed a volunteer helper and are roughly mounting him. Along the sidelines more vacuums savagely smash into one another while their frantic owners try to pull them apart. The roar is deafening.

Their own vacuum breaks loose and lurches into the fray.

Disconnect! screams the trainer who's standing on a chair.

Plugs are pulled. Vacuum cleaners stop in mid-roar and there's a stunned silence. But after the vacuums are re-plugged the brawling resumes.

Hammers! screams the trainer. Now!

The object: to batter the vacuums into submission.

The assault works. Spluttering vacuum cleaners, some with missing wheels, all with dented casings, are dragged by their sweating handlers into the obedience ring. Training can now begin.

On the night before the last class the man and woman are awakened by their vacuum standing beside their bed.

What does it want? The woman whispers.

Maybe to get in bed with us, says the man. Maybe it's nervous about the obedience trials tomorrow.

Don't be insane, says the woman. I think it means to harm us. It wants to use its upholstery attachment to suck out our brains ...

What? Tonight? You mean tonight?

Omigod, cries the woman. I never thought ... You don't think? What if? What do we do? ... Maybe all along ... We've been so stupid ... To let such a thing into our home ... It's one of those psychopathic ones, isn't it? ... We've bought a psychopathic vacuum cleaner ... One of the twenty percent worldwide ... They have no human feeling ... It's that weird Swivel Glide Vision, isn't it? ... Wreaking havoc ... Breaking hearts ... Oh, it's too terrible ... I can't stand it ... I'm going to throw up ...

The vacuum continues to stand beside their bed. There's sweat and pounding hearts beneath the covers.

Maybe I can make a break for the hammer, says the man.

What? And leave me here?

It's on the kitchen counter ...

You—are—not—leaving—me—here ... alone ... with the vacuum cleaner ...

Then we'll go together, says the man. On the count of three I'll fling the covers over the vacuum's head.

Its head?

Its thingy. Its neck.

Then what?

We'll make a run for it. I'll get the hammer. Then kill it ...

I'll get the axe, says the woman.

Okay, says the man, I'll start counting. One. Two. Three.
Now!

# THE COFFIN GURU

A woman spends several years lying in a coffin watching TV. She's grey-faced and bloated like a new corpse. She's a Coffin Guru.

The coffin is propped up in the woman's living room. On a side table sits a pot of chamomile tea. The tea, she says, keeps her calm.

Many people visit the Coffin Guru because they believe they are living in End Times and that she has important things to say.

Today her subject is the invention of the immune system.

It's something we've dreamed up, she croaks to her followers during a pause in her viewing. An invisible shield that supposedly lives inside our bodies and protects us from death ... It's the way we've solved the dilemma of having become gods ourselves ... We being the powerful destroyers of the planet ... And since we gods are really humans we had to think up a way to kill us off ... Enter the immune system ... A mental trick we use to convince ourselves that death's a self-driven punishment ... And here comes the part that dupes us ... The part that makes us hope for a present kind of immortality ... Because there's a slim chance that some of us possess a top-of-the-line model ... Meaning good genetics ... Which then means we can go around boasting like stupids that our immune systems are indestructible and that we're safe, protected ... But guess what? ... It ends up the same old story ... Each of us in a wheelbarrow over there at the dump ... The paranoid psychotics were right ... If you want protection you might as well line your walls and ceilings with tinfoil ... Or for solace watch reruns of *I Love Lucy*—all those happy dead people getting up to the damnedest things ...

Sermon over, she scrolls the channels: a weatherman at a map, a woman's hand covered in soap suds; a car exploding; a fiftyish woman stirring ingredients into a glass bowl; two politicians giving a press conference; lion cubs wrestling on the sunny plains of Africa ...

The Coffin Guru's husband dreams of leaving his wife and moving to an ice floe in Greenland. He's attracted by Greenland's frozen waste—so white and still. He's found a book on the place.

He reads to the Coffin Guru: In Greenland, the icebergs are one million years old and three-quarters of the land is pure ice. It costs one hundred and fifty dollars a day to rent a dog sled. A helicopter costs two thousand dollars a day. That's because there're few roads in Greenland and reindeer are scarce. The rugged coastal areas offer the only foothold for human life ...

The Coffin Guru screams at her husband. Make me some tea!

He keeps reading. The average yearly precipitation in Greenland is less than ten inches. It's the world's largest island and—this is interesting—it's often called an Arctic desert ...

Shut up about Greenland!

There's a plant there, he continues unabashed, called Fluffy Artic Cotton Grass. It grows for two weeks during the summer. Each flower is made of white petals that are as delicate as feathers. He pauses. Think of it, precious—lying in a field of Arctic flowers ... instead of ...

Imbecile! There is no Greenland! Greenland's a dream! You haven't been listening? There is no escape ...

## SHIFT WORK

I got the call. I'd made the short list. The interview process was rigorous: role playing, essay writing, written tests. The executive type who did the hiring—forties, slicked-back hair, expensively dressed—revealed himself as the boss. He said, "This job. In so many words. Do you think you're able?"

"Yes," I said. "I'm able. I'm full of potential!" I got the job. I was thinking more about being potentially unemployed than giving good service, about the comfort of food and a good night's sleep.

I was given the graveyard shift, eleven to seven. With two fifteen-minute breaks and a thirty-minute "lunch" at three. It's true there was a good deal of sitting in the big chair waiting for the boss to appear. A good deal of vigil-keeping, as it were, staring into the night from the tenth-floor office, admiring the wash of city lights below.

But when the time came I was ready to act. When the office door opened and I saw the cocky grin on the boss's face, saw the swaggering, laughing, easy-going way he entered the room, I jumped him. This is what my job required. I jumped the boss and pinned him to the floor with my knees.

"Wipe that shit-eating grin off your face!" I cried via the memorized script. Using a damp, grease-smelling cloth I harshly rubbed his face. "What's so funny? You live in a funny world? While the rest of us are bruised and betrayed, polluted, diseased!"

Rubbing his face red until all hilarity was removed. You had to hand it to him. He knew when his unbounded joy of life was getting out of hand.

"Never forget," he would tell me afterwards by way of thanks. "When the time comes the man in the bright white nightgown comes calling."

And who's to argue? Right now a fleet of hearses awaits our business. The drivers are hidden behind darkened glass, but we know they're wearing white.

## THE EXPEDITION

Decked out in khaki shorts and pith helmets and carrying butterfly nets, they have mounted an expedition. They are curious: Where do all the lost minds go? Lost minds, they believe, are like butterflies disconnected from flowers.

Marching behind a flag that says *Reunion*, the expedition heads towards the local dump and the mountain there of kitchen sinks, TV sets, wet mattresses, and car parts. They expect to find lost minds blowing about the garbage—broken bits of memory, the odd disintegrating word.

En route, they pass an insane asylum. Behind barred windows black eyes stare at them from the mindless skulls of inmates. The expedition leader waves, calling, "Hold on! Won't be long now!"

The mouths of the inmates open. "Mama," they cry.

# A CERTAIN AGE

Having reached a certain age they decide to test creation. This involves liberating the household pets.

First—the cat is sent to Arizona for the warmth. The cat is arthritic, twenty-one years old.

How much time does the cat have left?

Good question.

How much longer should she be made to howl every time she moves?

Good question.

Scottsdale Arizona, mean temperature in the mid-eighties, will be just the thing for her old bones.

Mid-eighties—that's warm.

They have a friend there who wrote on his Christmas card: *Drop in any time!* A man who signs his Christmas card with love from him and his cats, putting the cats before his wife, they reason, would understand.

So why not? The cat is shipped UPS with a note: *Guess who's having a dream vacation?*

Next—the dog. It's his birthday. Fourteen years old.

That's old in dog years.

Real old.

They retire the dog. Throw out his collar and leash. Tell him to put up his feet: *Start a hobby! Enjoy yourself! These are your golden years!!*

A senior dog.

There are homes for dogs like that. Twilight homes providing wheelchair walks, soft ice-cream.

No—the dog stays. They love the dog—flatulence, food fixation, senility, all of it.

They don't love the aged rabbits. Never have. The rabbits are another story. Coal and Snowball. They're carted outside and placed in the middle of the back lawn, there to scamper off to Mr. Macgregor's garden. Not to be. The rabbits exhibit agoraphobia. Scream when a cloud passes overhead. The rabbits are tranquilized and returned to their cage.

Finally, the canary.

Ceremonially, the birdcage is placed on the front porch. A few crows alight on nearby trees to watch. The cage door is opened. They bend close to the canary and whisper nervously: *This is it! Freedom! At last!*

The canary refuses to budge. Clings to the cage bars twittering hysterically.

The canary is the final sign. Because when a canary screams at freedom it means you can cling to creation for a few more years. But you must be careful, especially if your combined ages add up to more than one hundred years.

That's old in human years.

Real old.

They go back inside and bolt the door.

# OLD

He has hit the wall and the watch is on. The signs are unmistakable: the speech meant to raze, the assumptions levelled. The point comes, he says, when your eyes stay permanently open; everything, even the content of your dreams, becomes framed by your imminent demise; there's a flattening out— the flow steadies; you no longer are a river of energy; you are a softly ebbing sea. About being unwanted, he says, that is to be expected; death is a demographics of attitude, as Breugel saw, the high and the low brought together in an agony of last moments. Theories, he says, do not help; especially Einstein's which has been wrinkled and twisted so that relativity has become one more hopeless vision. Now he asks a final question: Who will keep up the hollering about this monstrous life?

We are heartsick, and believe it is kinder to keep these things to yourself. The here and now is difficult enough; we don't want to be reminded about what lies ahead.

We are thinking of ways to silence his tongue.

Pills, probably.

# RIDE

I was in a crowd rushing for a seat on the helicopter.

When everyone was seated I spoke to the stranger beside me. "Is this the way you die? Is this how it's done? Hurrying off for a helicopter ride?"

"Death's free," the man said. "That's all I know."

He wasn't old, perhaps fifty, and wore a rumpled brown suit.

The senior citizen on my other side said, "At least you don't have to save up for the ride, take out a loan, or use your credit card. When the time comes you get the ride money or no money. And since we're poor the government takes care of us."

I wondered why everyone looked so happy. Judging by their pink faces you'd think we were departing on a dream vacation.

By now the helicopter blades were turning. I noticed that the windows in our compartment spanned a full three hundred and sixty degrees. The view would be spectacular.

I spoke to the senior citizen who seemed to know so much. "How long is the ride?"

"Not long," she said. "A quick ascent, a breathtaking look at the scenery."

"And then?"

"And then it will be over."

"How will it occur?"

"Each according to their makeup," she said. "But afterwards we'll be dumped in the sea."

## INTERSECTION

They'd been wandering about on the freeway divide for several hours and finally came to an intersection. Mid-day, it was empty. The sun was hot; everything was sharp angles, still. Suddenly movement erupted and they became aware of many wild animals roaming about on the road and sidewalks, as if on a savannah. There was a hot wind now, dryness in their mouths. A Bengal tiger, beautiful but menacing, stopped in its pacing to stare at them. Insects were everywhere: spiders swayed on threads from light posts; there were puddles of ants on the road. Overhead, large birds with curved yellow beaks rode the air like gloomy scouts. Further off, they saw a gate— the entrance littered with corpses.

This wasn't a jungle, or a zoo.

Soon enough they understood that they were dead—shades in a fearsome underworld.

Still, something propelled them towards the gate. Perhaps it was the entrance to their usual world. Perhaps they could return ...

A flea the size of a pickup truck barred their way ...

## POOF

A doctor tells a woman during her regular checkup that her black hole is getting larger. Each of us possesses a black hole, he says, because each of us resides in a separate universe. Eventually we disappear down our own black holes. Then, poof, we're gone! It's neat. It's tidy. It's basic science.

The woman does not share the doctor's delight. We are one universe, one brain, she says. We are a flock of humans. And I won't be disappearing, I'll be recycled. I'll be taking my place in the eternal white light. Thereafter to become who knows what? A worm, perhaps. A swan. Trust a male to come up with a black hole. That worn-out womb thing. That vagina-gobbling-you-up thing. Crawl back in a hole if you want to. Not me. I'm spring-boarding in a different direction.

Have it your way, says the doctor. But it's a proven fact. As we age our black holes get larger. The universe is all about black holes.

Gobble, gobble, gobble, says the woman.

Just then a great black thing and a great white thing collide in the doctor's office and an even greater grey thing is born. It looks like a cloud of ashes.

My god! the doctor and the woman cry as they immediately age, whither, die, and disappear.

Imagine their surprise ...

# 3.

# A Talent for Subversion

# DEAR TARDY SUBSCRIBER

Curious to see what your old friend Sally from elementary school is doing? Well, you can't. It's too late. She's dead. If you had taken out a subscription to *ClassFind* when we first contacted you, you might have known. Might have had one last human connection with Sally. But you didn't and it's too bad. Now you'll never be forgiven for locking her in the bathroom in grade four. The girl who hated the birthday present you gave her. We were as shocked as anyone to hear what you had done. No one expects to be locked in the bathroom on their special day while everyone else tears around outside chasing balloons and eating cake and not noticing their absence and not being excited about their birth. No one is ever led to believe that such a thing could happen to them. But it happened to Sally. And you're to blame. It was one of those doors that can be locked from outside. You said, Come here, Sally, see what I've got! Then ran out locking her in the bathroom. Now you'll never have the chance to beg her forgiveness. Not that she would have forgiven you. Her mother never forgave you. She said at the time, That girl ought to be smothered. And ordered you out of her house. We know all this because *ClassFind* asks subscribers to provide their life story for the interest of other subscribers. Sally told us her story, named names—*your* name. How the present was a "stupid worm ornament" and asked what kind of a present is that? We have to agree with her in light of your behaviour. Who gives an ornament of a worm as a birthday present? No one decent, that's who. Only warped, twisted weirdoes, that's who. But we'll give you a chance to redeem yourself. We'll make a special allowance. Take out a subscription to *ClassFind*. Tell your side of the story. Maybe Sally deserved what she got. Maybe giving her a worm ornament was an inspired gesture. A subscription to *ClassFind* is the only way you'll achieve peace of mind about the birthday incident at Sally's. You'll have the opportunity to tell your surviving classmates from elementary school that you're sorry. The opportunity to finally blubber and grovel, to demonstrate some raw pain and emotion about the reprehensible event.

Sally and her mother are on haunting standby. Should you decline our offer they will take the form of seventy-one-year-old women wearing canary yellow T-shirts and they will sabotage your workout at the gym. They'll be randomly fiddling with the controls on the weight machines and the treadmill. As a result, you will break your arms, your legs, and your neck. Splendidly, your gift-giving days will be over.

# BAD BOY

My husband hides lethal chemicals the way some men hide pornography, guns, or a bad drinking problem. When I discovered a sealed box of Diazinon lodged inside the toilet tank, I became suspicious and asked him about it. "Guilty," he said, and went on to tell me about his club which is called Chemical Men. He said he hoped I'd understand.

He's belonged to the club for eleven years. It's a secret club, which is always the best kind, my husband says, a club dedicated to the preservation of antique chemicals. Members collect DDT, napalm, and unopened cans of Raid from the middle part of the last century, and then they trade these items, or sell them. They have a monthly Internet newsletter and, each autumn, an underground festival which is virtual but well attended. According to my husband, members of the club are especially interested in the uses of industrial chemicals for the home garden.

This past week my husband says he'd been involved in an Internet bidding war over a vial of Agent Orange. It's been exciting for him, he says, and is relieved, now, to be able to share this excitement with me. So far he hasn't had a winning bid, but he's hopeful. Apparently, collecting lethal chemicals has become a hobby for him; much like the hobby his father had which was collecting silver foil from cigarette packages. His father, who'd spent his working life as a travelling salesman for Bic Pens, rolled the foil into balls the size of basketballs. No one is sure why he did this, other than for the calm it gave him. When he died, five silver balls were bequeathed to my husband, representing an adult life of smoking, collecting foil, and single-minded rolling. Curiously my father-in-law did not die of lung cancer, but of old age.

My husband is quick to point out that besides the benefits of engaging in a hobby—old age not withstanding—collecting lethal chemicals is important archival work. Like his father, he looks upon his collection as something to leave the kids. "In fifty years' time do you know what these babies will be worth?" he asks, referring to his stockpile, now covering a quarter of the garage floor after retrieval from the several hiding places around the house and yard—inside the old croquet bag; above the ceiling tiles in our son's former bedroom; behind the hot water tank in the laundry room; within a specially designed space in the wood pile.

My husband is gleeful telling me this, but I suspect that his glee has more to do with hoodwinking me for eleven years than in leaving a legacy for the kids. Eleven years ago I declared our property a chemical-free zone. All herbicides and pesticides were banned. "Here is a corner of the world that will remain free of contamination," I said. I was proud of my stand and told our neighbours, the retired psychiatrist and his wife. Now I'm remembering how they were taken aback with the news but quickly recovered to register blank agreement. I'm also remembering how over the years I've seen them—usually at dusk—creeping between their rows of tomato plants wearing face masks and carrying buckets and spray nozzles. For some reason I didn't associate this behaviour with the use of lethal chemicals; I'd assumed they were using something safe like soap suds. It's obvious now what they were doing, heedless of soil contamination in their quest for massive tomatoes. My husband has now confirmed that they are also members of Chemical Men.

I am convinced that my husband has been dipping into his collection. The slugs in the garden did not pack up and move of their own volition. I realize this now. Before then our yard was a maze of weeds, grasses, wild flowers, and rangy, creeping roses instead of the monster-size flowers we have now. By all accounts, they should be bug-eaten and straggly. I thought these vibrant over-bloomers grew without much effort other than admiring them and pulling the odd weed. I thought they had achieved balance with the natural world and that they were, in fact, thriving in a happy, chemical-free way. Obviously, I was wrong.

Still, I have to acknowledge my husband's ability to carry off his eleven-year practical joke. The thrill he had while hoodwinking me must have been enormous, not to mention the secret fun he's had when I gushed over the wisteria blooms, or the creeping veronica, or the profusion of tulips, and so forth. No doubt the psychiatrist and his wife were in on the joke.

Registering my dismay, my husband claims that he used the chemicals because of me; that it was an act of love because I enjoy continual bloom in a plant and am saddest in winter when there is only holly and snowberry to look at. But there is nothing sadder than a man armed with a canister of herbicide and a battery-powered light strapped to his head while sneaking about the yard at midnight and I am not even slightly convinced. My husband is not a violent man but I think the thrill he gets from handling the destruction that resides in lethal chemicals must be overwhelming. This thrill, coupled with the thrill of hoodwinking me, further produces in him a feeling of euphoria; he's being a bad boy when he does this. I think at heart that this is what my husband is—a bad boy who has got away with things.

Fortunately, I am a good girl. And I am reasonable. I have given him twenty-four hours to begin the detoxification process that will return our yard to its essential condition of weeds and dead things. I am not saying *or else*. I am not saying I will pack my bags and become my own hobby tomato. I am saying, "Just because some of us can read and write and do a little math, that doesn't mean we deserve to conquer the universe."

# FUNNY

Once, funny was everywhere. Grandmas went funny, rocking in out-of-the-way corners, conversing with flies. Men's eyes went funny when they wanted sex, a cross-eyed leer meaning wives could kiss the day goodbye. Anything in a kitchen could smell funny—meat, milk, fish—and cause you to hold your nose and scream. Or a body could smell funny—B.O., farts, poop. If you had buck teeth or elephant ears you went to the back of the line because you were funny-looking and of no use to a living soul. If you had a queer streak you were told to stay home from school because there was something funny about you—and a good chance you'd turn into an axe murderer. If you were really crazy and pulled your pants down on Cordova Bay Road like Mr. Sharp did and waved your thing at passing cars you were put in the funny farm no questions asked. Some people had a funny bone, and some, like Mrs. Sharp, did not. With your friends, all you wanted was to crack people up, get the last laugh, laugh your head off, be the life of the party, die laughing.

Once, teachers warned never to pull a chair from a person in the act of sitting—they could break their backs. You did it anyway. The harder they fell, the better you laughed. At home, if you were caught laughing behind someone's back, you were asked, "What's so funny?" If you smirked and said, "Nothing," you were told to wipe that smile off your face. If you took your own hand and dragged it across your mouth, you could count on hearing, "You think that's funny? I'll show you what's funny!" And be shoved outside to face a row of marigolds and weeding.

Once, you practised slap-stick chaos. You were Larry, Curly, or Moe and went around sticking fingers in people's eyes, bonking heads with pretend two-by-fours. Or you impersonated Ed Sullivan, calling him old stone face. You thrust out your hips, put your hand on your chin, and said, "Welcome to the shew. And, now—in the audience—direct from the Palace Theatre in Las Vegas—the Queen of England! Stand up and take a bow, Queenie!"

You couldn't give it up. Funny followed you down the years. Now, you've moved on to pets. Pets are good for a laugh. You dress the cat in doll's clothes to amuse your wife. You make a sandwich by wrapping bread and butter around the dog's tail and watch your kids bust a gut. You dye the fur of a caged rabbit sky blue and tell everyone it's art. Lately, you've been sneaking in a mate for the pet mouse and watching them go at it like a pair of tiny machines gone crazy. You do this alone, at night with a flashlight, absorbed with watching, feeling strangely full of hope ...

## HAPPY BIRTHDAY

*For George Bowering*

I had a baby but it refused me, was not interested in nursing, made no demands. I put it in a closet, in its carrying cot, and when I went to get it, it was gone. The baby was a girl. Briefly, I was upset, panicked, ran looking for help, someone to report to. Ultimately it was to my sister-in-law. She'd moved the baby to another cupboard. "I need that cupboard for towels," she said. It was her cupboard, her towels. Soon after I left my sister-in-law's house. Put the baby into the back seat of the station wagon. Even though the baby still made no demands, I worried she might be hungry and stopped to nurse. She turned her head away. Clearly we were not bonding though I had tried. At home my husband said, "It's hormones, or you're a klutz, or who knows?" Then he lit my right nipple. My right nipple was a candle wick. In fact, I had five nipples located down my right front like a dog's. My husband lit all five. "Got to celebrate something," he said. But what? Then I remembered. Your birthday! Now I am back in the station wagon driving around with five burning nipples, your Happy Birthday song still sweet on my lips, and a baby who won't give me the time of day. But here's the thing: because of those nipples you get to make one birthday wish.

# A UNIVERSE RUNS THROUGH HIM

I gave a writing class to a group in the city. It was held one evening in the basement of a library. The idea was that I would provide writing exercises, and talk about the craft. Thirteen people were in attendance, among them an eighty-eight-year-old man who had just self-published his twelfth book—*Travel Tales*. "It's about my thirty years in the travel business," he told the group when it was his turn during introductions. "An insider's view. Things you'd never suspect that go on behind the scenes." He had copies with him for sale.

Another student, a woman, said she had written a book on management skills and was interested in who my agent was. A shy Chinese woman said she came to the class because she was stuck in the house all day and needed something to do. A woman, who kept her coat on and her purse on her lap, said she was attending as support for her husband who wanted to write westerns. He sat next to her, tilted back in his chair, a fleshy, middle-aged man with a pencil stuck behind his ear.

While the participants worked on the first exercise— "Details from Your Childhood"—the supporting wife stared grimly over her husband's shoulder at what he was writing. Beside them an elderly couple took turns with a pen writing on the same sheet of paper. After completing the exercise, the woman told the group that she and her husband had gone to elementary school together and so shared the same childhoods. Her husband, a thin man in an oversized blue sweatshirt that had "The Right Stuff" written in white across his chest, explained their unique writing style. "We do this all the time. The wife writes the beginning of sentences and I write the end. I'm better at ends than she is."

I told the group we would now do an exercise called "Stretching the Commonplace; Blowing off the Dust." "It's about using the imagination," I said, and explained that I would provide them with a first sentence—something provocative or startling. They would then write the next sentence, and the next, moving on to paragraphs if they felt inspired. To get them going and to give them an idea of how wonderful such writing could be, I read aloud a poem by bill bissett. It began: *god or th goddess as yu like 2 say is a giant / child leening against a giant window sill / looking out at rolling emerald hills th shining / turquoise watr brite yello zaneeness birds evree / wher lifting melodeez...*

When I had finished I said, "A writer like bill bissett has the doors wide open all the time. A universe runs through him. bill bissett," I said, "is in a permanent state of wonder, perfectly attuned to the swirl of life within and beyond him."

The man with the supporting wife scoffed, and said, "What's he on?"

Several people laughed.

The three sentences I gave the class to choose from were: "My mother ate cats"; "I had charge of an insane asylum, and I was insane"; and "They have lost the baby down the sewer." They had ten minutes. Then everyone shared what they had written.

Of the thirteen people in the class, eleven, including the elderly couple, had chosen sentence number one about the mother who ate cats. The shy Chinese woman chose sentence number three about losing the baby down the sewer. "We went crazy with fear," she wrote. When it was his turn to read, the man with the watching wife smirked, folded his arms across his chest, and said, "Pass."

I then talked about dreams and the other places imaginative material might be found. "It's important not to get stuck in habitual grooves," I said, thinking fondly of bill bissett. Some of the students wrote this down.

At the end of the class, the man with the watching wife explained to everyone the proper way to sit in a chair. He said there should never be wrinkles in your wrists when you work at the computer, and that the computer screen should be blue, not white. He said you should get up every twenty minutes and walk around. "Move the blood. Otherwise it pools." He said he was an expert in ergonomics, that's what he did for a living.

For all this I was paid fifty dollars. The next day I took another trip to the city. I planned to spend the money at second-hand stores. I was looking for a winter sweater. Also, I needed some brite yello zaneeness.

# FINE, THANK YOU

I retrieved my impounded 1982 Chevette from the local towing company. This is a business that for some reason employs only fat young people and they all came out to watch while the holding pen—"the cage" as it is called—was unlocked by a boy with two massive chins. It seemed to be a ceremony for the employees, this unlocking of the cage, and they trailed behind me in silence and condemnation, all of them wearing grey uniforms with their names written in red above the breast pocket—Justin, Michelle, Amy, Kevin.

Their demeanour shouldn't have been surprising, though, because they'd lived with my impounded car for the last month, guarding it, doing the paper work, and, most certainly, reading the police report which stated that my nineteen-year-old daughter had driven my car while in possession of an invalid driver's licence. Naturally they would be curious about the owner, about the person who mismanaged her life—and her daughter—to such an extent that her car ended up here. Hence, the entourage. They had stories to tell, and I was one of them.

The four employees—office staff and dispatchers—waddled after me into the cage where about twenty impounded cars and trucks were randomly parked. A high wire fence surrounded the vehicles and the ground inside was muddy. Tall grass grew between some of the parked cars. Leaning against the far fence were the saddest cases, the rusting sedans and pickup trucks with flat tires, the ones that would never be claimed. My car was parked near the gate.

Earlier, I'd paid the four-hundred-dollar "impoundment fee" from my daughter's savings account to Amy, the larger female employee. But she couldn't find the car keys; they weren't on the pegboard behind her desk. She got flustered, then annoyed. "I just had them," she said crossly, searching everywhere. Finally Kevin and Michelle struggled off their stools and helped in the search. But they couldn't find the keys either. Luckily I had a spare set.

When I unlocked the car, I saw that the original keys were on the floor. I turned to the employees who were standing side by side watching me so intently, and laughed, "There are the keys! They were locked in the car all along!" No one said a word, cracked a smile, or indicated that they had even heard me. So I said it again. Finally, Justin, the boy with two chins, said quietly, "It's not hard to break into these cars. We could have done that if we had to." The others nodded grimly.

When the car started I looked over and saw what I thought was disappointment on the employees' faces. Perhaps this was the point of the ceremony: the satisfaction they'd get telling car owners about the additional fee to tow the car *out* of the cage.

I drove away and still they didn't move, just slowly turned their heads in unison and stared after me, sullen and superior. They were the good ones, they were telling me, solid, law-abiding. They had the backup of the government and the RCMP; they were weight and they had more weight behind them.

Driving the Chevette home and experiencing its particularities—a heater that didn't work, the tinny shudder the car gave when it hit a rut—I felt impounded by the employees' condemning gaze. I kept repeating to myself: We are *not* a dysfunctional family; we drive old cars because we don't believe in car payments; our daughter is learning an important lesson about driving with an invalid driver's licence; eventually the light will dawn; eventually we will no longer be involved in her mistakes.

You have to believe in certain things. Each day you write a script for yourself. It's like a horoscope; you describe yourself to yourself. We are clean and decent people, we say, but we prefer old cars. And we love our children. We do what we can for them because our children are as awkward and stupid and impulsive as we once were. But all this will pass. One day they'll be middle-aged and visit us in the assisted living centre bringing treats—chocolates, pizza, and a certain red wine we're fond of. After the visit, we'll sit on the clematis-covered veranda with blankets spread across our knees, sipping the wine, and watch our children with their thinning hair drive away in their old cars. We'll be feeling a sense of accomplishment about them, and pride that we've successfully imparted our values to them about old cars and good wine, about driving with a valid driver's licence. Some time later an attendant might ask us how we are.

"Fine," we'll answer. "Thank you."

# THANKS TO GEORGE INKWELL

I have a conversation with George Inkwell, the famous breast historian. The occasion is a reception in his honour.

George Inkwell is tall, cadaverous-looking, and has a prominent nose. During our conversation he leans forward and strokes my breasts, all the while lamenting, "It's a shame the breast has become so hidden during this age. We've had thousands of years of civilized breasts nourishing the species in all and every manner, and now the practice is to hide them away. Breasts should be served on a plate and celebrated."

He sighs. It's difficult for him to properly stroke my breasts because, as usual, they're encased—first in a sheath of elastic, then in layers of cotton and wool. To please George Inkwell, I unbind them and arrange them on a dinner plate that also acts as a tray for my glass of wine. Soon other women do the same thing—breasts of all sizes are served up for George Inkwell's historic appreciation.

He roams the reception room gawking and smiling ...


Thanks to George Inkwell I've discovered my life's work. I will become a pioneer—a penis historian. Even though I am small, anonymous-looking, and unlikely to command attention— which incidentally is the description of many pioneers—I will visit public gatherings with my bullhorn and holler, "You men might like to untangle your penises from the bowels of your boxers!"

I may be carted away as a maniac, but I won't be deterred. Following George Inkwell's lead, I will compile a scholarly work on my subject. Eventually there will be acclaim and parties in my honour.

"Penises could do with some fresh air after all the centuries they've been hidden away like worms!" I'll tell my audiences jovially. At which point penises of all sizes will swing free through trouser fronts. Penis Flopping will become the fashion craze that culminates my life's work and ...

Women and children, dogs and forgotten grannies will roam the streets of our cities gawking and smiling ...

# LEAKING MEN

There is a thin young man with long hair who knows poetry and music but must be confined to his room because of a bowel problem. He could be a lover except for the bowel problem. There is an older man in his forties who suffers from a seeping mind. He can't hold his thoughts. No sooner does he have a thought than it liquefies and dribbles away. Because of this he's constantly agitated. He also would be an unsuitable lover.

Still, I have allowed these men to live in my house. I have rented out the two basement rooms because I am short of money, nothing new for me. I use the words "mild," "very," and "appalling" to describe how short of money I can be. When the state reaches "appalling" I put up a notice.

Then money changes hands. This is always a joy and a relief. Yet there is a cost to my newfound comfort: I become my tenant's caretaker. This has happened with the two leaking men. Not only do I prepare special meals for them and see to their linen, but each Monday I load them into my car and take them for a drive. It's a chance for them to see more of the world than their quiet rooms allow, and a chance for me to earn extra money. I usually take them to the ocean to look at the waves and the shore birds.

I am fond of the ocean. Most evenings I walk to the small beach near my house in hopes of meeting Smokey, a man who can't stay in his own body but leaks into other bodies, usually a cat. Smokey is beautiful, furry or plain, cat or man. This is why I keep so many cats, and why I often need money—for their food and vet bills. Whenever a cat jumps on my lap purring, I ask, "Smokey? Is that you?"

Smokey keeps my mind on the good, bad, or indifferent present. I am prone to leakage myself ...

## WHEN THE BUDGIE RESCUED THE PARTY

The music was wrong—irritating. Every CD had been heard
before. The pre-dinner talk was halting; there were silences,
yawns. When it came to the meal, the seven-hours-in-the-
making yam soup was eaten without comment; the salad
avocado was unripe. The main course was problematic
because the plates warming in the oven overheated, making it
impossible to pick them up without gloves. The plates sat
cooling on the table while the food on the buffet lost heat.
Soon enough the truth about the main course was revealed:
the chicken breasts were dry; the potatoes were dry *and* boring;
the steamed kale was limp, so overcooked it tasted slimy.
There should have been gravy but there wasn't and the guests
asked for water. At dessert the bakery cookies were hard.
Dunking them in coffee didn't help. The guests gnawed on
the cookies, sighed, and looked towards the door. This was
when the budgie rescued the party. We let the budgie out of
its cage and told the story about him being overweight. We
pointed to the budgie and said he looked like a Rotarian with
a beer belly. The budgie flew by the dining room table wheez-
ing and the guests laughed. Like a blue-feathered Rotarian
only round like an orange, we said. The guests laughed some
more. What's his name? said the husband. Andy, we said,
after Warhol. That's rich, said the wife. And when he landed
on the table she said, Here Andy, but the bird ignored her.
Then she commented on the budgie's yellow stick legs, that
they looked absurd for a fat budgie, and how you couldn't see
his eyes for feathers. The husband said he'd never seen a fat
budgie before and asked how fat we thought it was in terms of

pounds—make that oùnces? We said we didn't know because we hadn't weighed him but said he was so fat he looked like a Buddha. The wife laughed at that and said Andy the Flying Buddha. She said the budgie wouldn't have a problem emptying his bird brain to achieve nirvana would he because there was nothing in his head? She said his brain must be the size of a grain of sand—knock knock, nothing there. Other than endlessly repeating peck peck peck like a Warhol print, said her husband and they both laughed loudly. We took exception. No, we said, the budgie's smart; he's on the Bird Watchers Diet—no suet, a teaspoon of birdseed a day. We told them how the budgie was p.o.'ed with the reduced meals and started catching flies and scrounging crumbs off the kitchen floor. We said he was on the diet because we were worried about his fatty heart and here the husband laughed and said, Imagine his heart bursting, imagine the budgie exploding in mid-air—kapow! Feathers and bits of Andy would be everywhere, said the wife, wiping her eyes. Actually how big is a budgie's heart? asked the husband. Probably the same size as his brain, said his wife. And when we didn't say anything there was an uncomfortable silence until we said, He's a cute little guy. Then the budgie flew by the table again. Off towards the kitchen, we said, reviving things, gone to throw himself against the fridge. Next we showed the guests the budgie's miniature weights—they looked like metal twigs. We said we were helping him get back in shape by exercising him regularly—lifting weights and letting him fly about the house as he was doing now, stopping every now and then to cling to the curtains and catch his breath. When he landed on the dinner table again he waddled across to the plate of hard cookies and started pecking at one but couldn't break through. My god, cried the wife, he'll break his beak! Quiet, said her husband, let's see what happens next. But other than poop on a dessert plate not much happened. When the guests were leaving they said thanks for a great evening, your budgie's a scream. Encouraged, we said, Wait till you see Roy our fat gerbil—he's thirty-four pounds. Oh, we've got one of those, said the wife—Amanda—she's on insulin. For fun pets, said the husband, you should meet our friends the Driscolls. They've got a herd of miniature rhinos no bigger than flies. After dinner they bring them out and let them stampede across the table—now that'll knock your socks off. But, seriously, folks, a fat gerbil just isn't in the same league as miniature rhinos. We found that out the hard way, the husband said, and looked at his wife, didn't we honey? But didn't elaborate on what must have been a shamefaced experience. After they left we found the budgie and removed his fat suit via the tiny zipper along his belly. He emerged sleek and yellow and flew off towards his cage. Good job, Sparky, we called after him, but felt defeated. Obviously, rescuing a dinner party with a fat budgie couldn't be tried again. Word would get out—fat budgies were now passé. So what else? Then we had it. We'll teach Sparky to sing something unusual. Or, better yet, give a speech. That would be hilarious. Something by Winston Churchill or Billy Graham. And during the party we'd call him Dale—after Carnegie ...

## BUDGIE SUICIDE

We don't know why he did it. He must have been unhappy. It can't have been easy for him—pecking the bell, hanging about on the pole, staring at the free birds outside the window, the robins, the gulls. Then every night the cage covered with a smelly dish towel. We wonder now if he'd been lonely for his own kind. Maybe he was pining for some squawky budgie sex. We wonder, too, at the strangeness of caging small birds. Like imprisoned souls, my mother-in-law once said.

Day after day we'd watch the budgie hopping along the pole, cocking his head at our huge cratered faces pressed against the cage. Cheep, cheep, cheep, we'd sing, and then scream happily when he paused, seemingly in communication.

We found him hanging from the bell. He had somehow wrapped the bell cord around his neck.

We wonder if our monstrous singing drove him mad.

# FUNERAL

We held a funeral for the budgie. I wrapped it in a handkerchief then dug a hole between the marigolds at the side of the house. My husband had said, Flush it down the toilet. It's dead. Get rid of it. But I wanted a proper funeral. I thought I might experience something grand.

I placed the handkerchief in the hole then covered it over. It was a cold afternoon, light rain. Hundreds of birds were perched in the fir trees that border our yard—crows, gulls, and smaller chirping birds. We stared at the mound. No one knew what to say. Finally I said, Poor Harry, and the children and I sobbed. When my husband pulled out his imaginary violin and started to play, the birds sent up a terrific screech, flapping their wings, causing the trees to tremble. A budgie requiem, thunderous, there in the rain.

At last, something grand.

# THE TAMING OF MRS. DUCK

My uncle once trained a budgie named Joey to take a piece of bread from his lips. It was a delicate manoeuvre—the bread offered through the cage bars; the budgie hopping along the pole to receive it; the intimate union between the two. He'd given the budgie to his shrewish wife as a peace-keeping gesture, hoping, perhaps, that she'd allow him to return to their bed. For several months he'd been banished to the pullout downstairs. Winter was coming and the basement room was drafty.

My uncle was a gentle man though many at the time called him a henpecked weakling. Every day after work as janitor at the public library—and after offering Joey a piece of bread—he'd watch cartoons on TV. His favourite cartoon was *Daffy Duck Gets Married*, a frequent repeat on Fun-O-Rama. I often watched it with him. He must have regarded the cartoon as the true story of his life with my aunt. Watching it, his breathing relaxed; he'd let his cigarette burn away in the ashtray. The cartoon's message seemed deeply meaningful to him.

The story was this: The lovable, fluffy, yellow duck that Daffy Duck had courted turns, immediately upon marriage, into a fat, chocolate-eating, nail-polishing, movie magazine—reading harpy. Daffy is shocked and tries, to no avail, to appease his bride with flowers and more chocolates in the hope that she'll return to the sweet duck he married. But the harpy won't have it. She throws the flowers at him, and screams for a bigger box of chocolates. Daffy is soon driven from home by her increasing demands and made to work like a slave; he's continually screamed at and hectored; the longer he's married, the fatter his wife becomes; soon the house is not big enough to contain her; then there's a brood of chicks that she refuses to look after; poor Daffy, as well as working two jobs, has to change diapers and fill baby bottles; he's run off his web feet; it gets worse and worse; his wife's demands increase; there's no satisfying the horror that is Mrs. Duck; she demands a mink coat, a diamond necklace, a Cadillac car. My uncle loved the part near the end of the cartoon when, like a miracle, Daffy wakes up. It has all been a bad dream, a nightmare of gigantic proportions. None of this has really happened! The relief Daffy experiences is enormous. He falls to the ground and kisses it; his little duck tail vibrates with joy. Life is again worth living. He raises his arms to the heavens and weeps with gratitude. Torment is a thing of the past. His death sentence has been revoked. There never was a Mrs. Duck. Daffy is a bachelor; he can stay a bachelor—forever! He can fluff up his feathers and dance. Or, if the fancy strikes him, put up his feet and watch the ball game on TV and feast on a mountain of hamburgers. He can live in splendid squalor. He will never again have to fix the kitchen sink—or anything else—on command. No female duck will ever scream at him again. He's free! Really and truly free!

"Oh, boy," my uncle often said when the cartoon was over. "That's one lucky duck."

Perhaps in sympathy with all caged animals, he often let Joey fly free within the house. It was a practice that resulted in the bird's untimely death. We can only imagine what happened. Attracted to the shininess of a razor blade left on my aunt's sewing machine, he must have flown down to inspect it and tried to pick it up with his beak. My uncle found him lying in a pool of blood and wept.

The bird's death marked a change in my uncle's personality. After that, he began asserting himself. Razor blades were banned from the house. He returned to the marriage bed without being asked. He took to calling his wife Mrs. Duck, smirking whenever he said this. He "turned a deaf ear" to her continual demands to perform household jobs: build her a new barbecue, fix the gutters, paint the living room. Finally, like Daffy Duck who understood deliverance, when my uncle retired he refused to budge from the TV set; he became fat and the house fell into disrepair.

In its own modest way my aunt and uncle's marriage had turned into *The Taming of Mrs. Duck* as, year after year, my aunt became increasingly nervous, more and more acquiescent. Even in widowhood, she hid her razor blades. When she died we found a small package of them—some new, some rusty— shoved beneath her mattress. My uncle, though, was remembered as a good man who loved all pets.

# EVER AFTER

## Session One

Prince Charming was giving a series of workshops. The first one was called "Converting Your Household Furniture to Foot Fetish Equipment." We have a strong interest in shoes and so attended because we admire the glass slipper master and wanted to learn some new (and possibly secret) skills from him.

Before beginning work, he told us the story. How he chose Cinderella's feet from all the other maidenly feet in the kingdom. How her feet had been the tiniest, and the smoothest, with high arches, and ankles as sharp as knives. How over the years he had moved on from glass slippers *exclusively*, and branched out into leather, canvas, and plastic. How the styles had expanded, as well, to include mules, pumps, boots, sling-backs, and thongs. How after what seemed like an eternity of marriage there were so many slippers they were housed in an entire castle room. How they were catalogued by colour and style from dressy to casual and that each shoe box had a Polaroid picture of its contents affixed to its lid. How over the years Cinderella's feet had flattened and she had grown claws and bunions but that the prince could still manage a tingle of excitement over her feet. How every once in a while he would holler throughout the castle, "C'mon Cinderella! Time to try on the slippers!" And off she'd trudge to the special room with the satin-covered stool for her to sit upon, and the embroidered cushion for the prince's knee as he bent before her trembling. How handling glass slippers made him feel like Prince Charming ...

Then we hauled out our wrenches, hammers, and lathes. Our project: convert a rocking chair into a claw-removal device ...

* * *

### Session Two

We signed up for session two—"Redecorating: From Dungeon to Ball Room"—because of what Prince Charming had done with the castle, which was now legendary. The way he'd dismantled the drawbridge and set about redecorating. Removed interior brick walls and covered the remaining walls with drywall and purple paint; boarded over the cold stone floors with hardwood; scattered patterned area rugs about; hung glitter balls from every ceiling; mounted bright yarn paintings in yellows, pinks, and lime greens; replaced the pokey, paranoid castle windows with a bank of picture windows. The way everyone had said throughout the centuries: What an artist! Look at the way he's opened up the castle! And then, as a final brilliant touch, the way he'd completely revamped the moat. Drained it. Sent the alligators packing. Filled it with earth and planted marigolds.

Love what you've done with the moat! people gushed.

During session two we engaged earth movers, dump trucks, and flag people. Our project: moat building for the suburban home.

* * *

## Session Three

"Converting Your Mother-in-Law into a Marble Buttress" was the title of the third session and it was so popular that many were turned away. Luckily we registered early. We were especially interested in this session because for part of it Prince Charming would be explaining the meaning that mothers-in-law—what he called Old Queens—have in our lives. And also since some of us were nearing Old Queendom ourselves we were curious about what to expect.

This session is like therapy, the prince told us and we nodded our heads because any discussion of human relations, as we have learned, contains an element of therapy.

He went on to explain that the first thing we would be doing is listing all the ownerships and accomplishments of our personal Old Queens. In this way we would know how to proceed because before the conversion of an Old Queen into a marble buttress can begin we must first understand our material. For example, said the prince, my Old Queen owns all the dolphins, sturgeons, and porpoises in the kingdom. She's conferred over 387,700 honours and awards, speaks fluent Freudian and often uses that language for audiences and state visits. As well she is the recipient of many unusual gifts, including jaguars and sloths from Brazil, beavers from Canada, and pineapples, eggs, a grove of mango trees, and seven kilograms of prawns from Jamaica. At Christmas she personally signs 37,500 Christmas cards and hands out 78,000 Christmas puddings to castle staff. She even has a hit CD—*Party at the Palace*—which sold over 100,000 copies in the first week of release and eventually went platinum ...

At this point those of us nearing Old Queendom dropped out. It was plain that our accomplishments and ownerships were nothing when compared to those of Prince Charming's Old Queen. We are made of lesser, dare we say, peasant stuff and could never provide enough raw material for a marble buttress. In fact we have come to the sad realization that our children would be hard pressed to even construct a straw effigy ...

* * *

### Session Four

By the fourth session attendance was down. But we showed up because we were curious what the title of this session would reveal—"Discovering 'Down the Hatch.'" Prince Charming began the class by handing out a bottle of red wine and a glass to each participant. Our project: to empty our bottles during the session by joining the prince in an ongoing toast.

Down the hatch! the prince cried, raising his glass. What a marvellous thing to say! he continued. A place of perpetual delight, as refreshing and as luminous as cool water. A place to have a few thoughts like an occasional cocktail, a few melt-in-your-mouth observations as substantial as meringues. Ah! Down the hatch! Cheers! What pleasure! To sit gaily with friends, laughing, talking ... I'd like a good draught of Down the Hatch on a steady basis.

By the end of the class we'd drained our bottles and were dancing. We had, as promised, discovered Down the Hatch and couldn't agree more with the prince's sentiments about what a delightful place it was proving to be.

* * *

## Session Five

The title of session five was "On Being Charming," but the big draw was a promised guest appearance by Cinderella. She was scheduled to talk about her enduring love of cleaning.

By way of introduction the prince said, The whole business of being charming lies in the notion of suspended life—arranging things so that our lives seem like a solid constant and we are never in a worried state about tomorrow. This is the beauty of a fairy tale—and we are all capable of creating our own fairy tales! Of making them as grand as a symphony! And what is it about symphonies?

What? What? we cried.

I'll tell you, said the prince. Symphonies are the world played large. Our puny worries reduced to a gust of wind. Harmony and a consonance of sound and heart ...

Phooey, we cried. Bring on Cinderella and her kitchen!

She arrived carrying a broom and wearing a grey apron, a plump, middle-aged woman with curly white hair. The prince, perhaps embarrassed by her appearance but definitely annoyed at our waning interest in him, sat petulantly at the side of the room and filed his nails while his wife spoke.

Cinderella said simply, charmingly, Nothing gives me more pleasure than cleaning. After years and years of castle life I am not ashamed to admit this. It is a joy and a relief to finally reveal that neither balls, nor parades, nor riding in pumpkins, nor wearing dresses made of stars, nor trying on glass slippers gives me as much pleasure as a job of cleaning. It's stadiums, the-atres, and streets after a parade that are my passions. It's the joy of watching a crowd drift away from a sporting event and knowing there'll be a fine mess left behind ...

Do you never remove your apron? we asked.

Only once a year in summer, Cinderella replied, when I take poesy of marigolds to the graves of the mice and songbirds that helped me so long ago. Otherwise I am happy to remain ever after with my cleaning. Sometimes I'd rather scrub a wall than have a thought ...

Everyone in the class agreed: Of the two, Cinderella was the more charming.

* * *

### Session Six

The final session was called "The Theory and Practice of Ever After."

Cinderella, with her passion for cleaning, with her seeming delight in the miracle of her own breath and skin, had given us hope that such a practice was possible. Our fears had become so great that we were skeptical that such a thing as Ever After even existed. The alarms that contributed to these fears were sounding hourly by then and we were never sure whether actual destruction was about to visit or if the alarms were merely a drill ...

Still, some of the more lighthearted, yet persevering, among us signed up for the last course.

Our project: construct a serviceable fairy tale, one that will result in our living happily Ever After.

# BACK THEN

I once had a job sleeping on city benches. It was a government job and the pay was good. Every evening I found a park bench or a bench at a bus stop and lay down. Back then sleeping on city benches was allowed. The government's idea was to have the working poor experience a few moments of illumination each morning when they passed by a sleeping figure, huddled and cold. In this way they might also experience relief and gratitude and thus the social hierarchy would remain intact.

Another job along the same lines, also government, was as a morale booster. My job was to wear brightly coloured clothes and walk the streets in the early morning, smiling and waving at people. Like sleeping on benches, smiling and waving at strangers did not mean the negative things it means today. Back then it meant cheerfulness, bell ringing, bonhomie. It meant a happy rousing of the troops, the start of another bright day.

At a later date, a corporation hired a number of us to act as sheepdogs. We were required to keep watch over the office workers who, before and after office hours, were running panic-stricken throughout the downtown core. Our job was to herd the workers to their building's elevators and eventually to their pens of safety where, once enclosed, they would become calm and attend to their work.

A more rewarding job came next. I became a judge. It was a growing field. Back then there were many areas of civil life that required judging. There were opportunities for a person with a fondness for rules to get ahead. And I had a fondness for rules, the harmless everyday rules that are the glue of a smoothly running society—rules of thumb, rules of the road, Robert's Rules of Order, rules of conduct. This quality, coupled with a clear certainty of purpose, made me a natural judge. I judged many things: school essays, poetry contests, property assessments, dog shows, shortbread at a craft fair, a beauty pageant—Miss Cowichan—and several talent nights. Back then the idea was to honour the beautiful in whatever form it took and, further, in the spirit of fairness, to give honourable mentions to all those who were never judged as winners. I dispensed thousands of ribbons that said "Nice Try," "Better Luck Next Time," and "You're a Winner Just by Being You!"

Years later I sold bets at the track. It was there that I received a hundred-dollar tip that turned me into a Pavlovian dog and caused me to hope for the future. That tip was an occupational hazard. Back then the future was considered a spiritual nonentity. And hoping for it—a sorrow beyond words.

## INSIDE THE WESTERN WORLD

The black family in the catalogue, all six of them, sits shoulder to shoulder in a 103 x 69 x 22–inch inflatable plastic pool. Mom, Dad, two boys, one girl, Grandma. The pool is situated beside a cedar fence. Beyond the fence the backdrop is sky-blue. Striped towels are spread across bright green Astroturf. Everyone in the pool is smiling, especially Grandma who has a rapt look on her face. She and the others gaze at the yellow plastic duck that the girl holds above her head like a sun. The pool costs $39.99.

On the next page two middle-aged white couples stand at an outside table. The scene is a casual afternoon party. Everyone wears Bermuda shorts, holds drinks in their hands, and appears to be pleasantly talking. There is a plate of cheese and crackers on the table. A three-foot-tall stainless steel Airworks Misting Fan is positioned like a quiet servant at the far left of the picture. It is an air conditioner for use on out-door patios. The caption says, *Simply attach to your garden hose.* The fan costs $99.99.

An Asian family is featured on a page about barbeques. The largest picture—the most expensive model—is of a woman and her two children. She and her daughter sit on deck chairs beside a large, black Centro Deluxe Barbeque which costs $399.99. Mother and daughter wear identical pink sweaters. They're looking fondly at the older child, a confident boy of perhaps eight, who is walking by holding a bowl of cherries. It is assumed that Father is away, absorbed with the business of

East/West fusion, perhaps working in electronics, or the commodities trade. In any case, his family enjoys the fruits of his labours, enjoys this Zen koan about success.

# PARADE

Some of us are hiding out at the dollar store while outside the gloominess of the world ...

Suddenly—a parade of dancing misfits! Giant laughing women with rouged cheeks; somersaulting midgets; winking old men skipping and jumping; human whirlwinds, male or female, you can't tell which; kids running along with swallows attached to strings like balloons; excited dogs wearing skirts; a priest with bells on his shoes ...

They're coming through the intersection, heading towards the far horizon. The music is loud—accordions, horns, drums, cymbals ...

A grinning man in a white suit saunters away from the parade and stops in front of the store. He beckons to me with a nod of his head.

My darling!

I rush outside.

He puts a finger to his lips as we head off—no words, no words ...

# A TALENT FOR SUBVERSION

There was an event at the community hall that brought in a lot of people. Coffee and cookies would be served after filling out a market survey. I attended because I'm a practitioner of random subversion. We sat in rows on metal chairs with clipboards on our laps and were given instructions by a boy in a business suit. When he was through talking I stood up and yelled, "Think what we're doing here, people! Nothing more than giving information to corporations so they'll know what to sell us!"

I'd hoped everyone would get up and leave, but no one moved.

A man called out, "I like filling out surveys. It's the only time I get to talk about myself!"

Some in the crowd nodded, some laughed. There were about two hundred people in the hall. I said to the woman next to me, "Really, we're nothing but slaves to the corporate world."

She smiled wearily. "Give it a rest, honey. Think of the coffee and cookies."

I sat there scrawling "no comment" beside each question. Later, at the refreshment table, people moved away from me.

I recognized the gesture. Being a subversive has that effect on people. The same thing happened at the drug store. I'd approached the makeup counter and spoken to the sales-clerks, a pair of elderly blondes. "Do you have any cream that gets rid of those horrible lines around your mouth?"

The women blanched and drew away. I thought they'd be amused by my no-nonsense attitude towards bodily decay—by my use of the word "horrible." They weren't.

One pointed to a small box on the shelf that had a price tag of $132.95. "We have this," she said.

"That's outrageous!" I cried, using my shrill subversive voice. "Most of that cost goes to corporate advertising! Don't you have any free samples?"

The women rolled their eyes.

My husband cited the above occurrences as examples of my failure to thrive in social situations. He pointed out that a talent for subversion will not land me a good seat at a dinner party. And, while I may argue that random subversion is morally important work, I had to admit he's right about the dinner parties.

We attended one last week. As usual, I was placed at the far end of the table. All the sharpest, brightest, so-called most interesting people—including my husband—were gathered at the other end. All the fun was happening down there—the witty conversations, the steady laughter—while I was seated far away gnawing on a celery stick.

Now and then I called out, "Hey, did you hear the one about the corporate takeover of our minds?" No one answered. I called out again. "Hey, you down there. You look like a beer commercial." No one paid the least attention.

The hostess, when she remembered, tended me like a volunteer worker for the useless. "More salt?" she asked. "Glass of water?"

If I strained I could hear what the interesting people were saying—"I just got back from a world tour." "How *is* the world?" "Subtle, very subtle."

But mostly I worked through the platter of celery, biding my time. Stared at the walls, looking for cracks.

## 4.

# Perpetual Coda

# NOVELS

They have written novels about bearing children; about exploding atoms; about not being weighted down by longing; about keeping meaning; about the blood theme against the inanimate; about sentiments formerly neglected; about imaginary horoscopes; about telling jokes; about grand-mothers seeking late-life sex; about posing ourselves mad like a Dali joke; about the consciousness of pet rats; about the barriers between heroic visions; about calm minds in chaotic times; about rebellion live and cracking; about the cool and the laughable; about the audience being an object of sexual desire; about the fantastic doomsday being neigh; about stretching out in our self-conscious beds; about love in the form of pirouetting dancers stopping by now and then to stroke our shoulders; about raging against the limitations of our minds; about enjoying the rosary of privilege; about the beseeching world of our hearts.

All this and it's only Tuesday ...

# A LITTLE SOMETHING

Fifty thousand vaginas were sent through the mail. Free samples. Part of an ad campaign for a revived play. We couldn't get ours open. It was shut tighter than a bivalve. "Useless!" My husband cried. "You call that a talking vagina?" I knew how he felt. Last week, a shrivelled penis was left on the doorstep. Another free sample. It came with a card: "A little something from the Goddess." Goddess is a line of lubricants. The penis was supposed to enlarge and chase you around the house and call you baby when rubbed with the cream. No dice. I couldn't even get it to squeak. The cream's a fraud. The penis lay on the dining room table like an old carrot. Then the cat dragged it off but gave up trying to chew it because the skin was so tough.

We've buried the vagina and the penis together in the back garden. Perhaps a little something might erupt through the dirt this spring.

# NEW ANGLES

She gives a reading in Montreal as part of a variety show. The performers include several jugglers, a mime, a comic, a number of teenaged dancers, and her—a literary reader. Her main rival is the comic. He has a projectile vomiting act in which he makes his words liquid and sprays the audience with pink-grey foam.

Why hasn't she thought of that?

People scream and duck but they don't leave the theatre. The comic gets laughs *and* a standing ovation.

What a dunce she's been! Projectile vomiting is brilliant.

Suddenly her act seems stale: A woman drags a suitcase across the stage, pulls letters from it, some as heavy as lead weights, then strings the letters together to form words, and then poems, stories, and novels of her own making.

Suddenly her act seems dull.

But what instead? Projectile vomiting as a new angle has been grabbed. What new angles are left?

Pull stories from a celestial clothesline so that the ceiling is pulled down as well while the audience gasps?

What? What?

The trials of the artist continue ...

## GREAT SOULS

We have friends who travel widely. China. Belize. England.
Italy. Australia. India. We, on the other hand, travel nowhere.
We do not consider ourselves uninteresting because of this
because we have read somewhere—in a psychology book about
archetypes, or perhaps it was a book on Zen—that it is possible
to be a great soul and never leave your back yard. We comfort
ourselves with this thought. We can be great souls, and interest-
ing, too, even though we do not have a constant and direct
experience of the wider world and its airports, hotels, museums,
unusual foods, differently dressed peoples, and warm oceans.

It is not necessary to travel widely to become a great soul.
We remind ourselves that this small West Coast world of ours,
this curious mix of paradise and dread, has interest enough,
beauty enough. It is by gazing upon the minutiae of everyday
life that a soul can swell and blossom into greatness, into the
sustained state of being here. Or so we believe. Over a dinner
of soup, bread, avocados, and rice we discuss these things.
And also what we would say to dinner guests, if we had them.
Instead of drifting off into travel and sleep we would suggest
that they might, like us, watch the micro-epics that are occur-
ring outside their windows every moment of every day. We, for
example, watch the changing weather. Because of this we have
become world citizens of interesting days. Partial sun.
Variable clouds. Light winds. Chance of rain. There is enough
weather to last a lifetime which is fortunate because this is how
we manage—eating and watching—our old wool cardigans
keeping our great souls warm.

# THE POET'S WIFE

The poet's wife is a saintly person. To keep body and soul together—to allow the poet to write his scintillating poems—she gives piano lessons to hemophiliacs. They love her instruction because she allows them to dispense with the pounding, fortissimo movements, allows them to brush the keys ever so slightly. And what results is a delicate, whispery music, bloodless, divine.

# A DAY SO HAPPY

*For Alma Lee*

I was washing my hands at the kitchen sink—music in the
background, some deeply cool jazz. It was six in the evening,
a night with friends stretching ahead—in honour of your
visit. Suddenly, a day so happy, like that poem by Czeslaw
Milosz—"Gift." You were outside, seated beneath the apple
tree, and shaded from the August sun, reading a book about
Scotland. The old dog slept at your feet. Butterflies perched
on the purple buddleia near where you sat. Not far from your
chair thousands of fat blackberries hung in clusters; you
could almost reach out and grab them. There was a slight
breeze stirring the poplars. Beyond the yard—the glittering
sea, a sailboat or two. "If this isn't paradise ... " you said,
coming inside for a drink before the guests arrived. You
and Terry and me. We toasted the hummingbirds that were
hovering over the feeder on the deck. We toasted the day and
the warmth of our friendship. "Totally superb. Totally solid,"
we said, quoting Dogen. We said it again and again that
night—August 9, 2003. There was something deeply fine ...

## DARKNESS IN THE ART

The convoluted nervous substance in her skull—it pounds. She's thinking about wattage and grave words of apology. About stories bumping along like refuse hauled in a three-wheeled cart. About the get-up-and-go metaphors, the ones that soar, that suggest the possibility of spinning it out. She's looking for these—the continuous sweep; the history of ourselves; a memory of amplified messages; a memory of requests; a memory of lightened hearts.

By day, this is her ball and chain—by night, her moon.

Please, she says, let's do something different.

Like what?

Try understanding instead of answers. Try believing each day is a marvel.

Oh that.

Meanwhile, every supper a last supper ...

Every thing a little broken down ...

Donald Barthelme stands nearby eating cheese.

"Don't fret, darling, it's only a poem."

## PLACE OF HONOUR

The hereditary chief of the local reserve had died. People shook their heads when they heard. On Friday he had been seen in the liquor store. On Saturday he was dead. No one expected the chief to die just then. He was ninety-two.

My friend who is eighty attended the two-day funeral. On Monday night there was a prayer meeting at the Shaker Church, and on Tuesday morning, the burial.

Three hundred people came. My friend was one of eight white men, a fishing friend of the chief's. Their friendship went back a long way and years ago they had made a pact that whoever died first would be the other's pallbearer. He had a place of honour at the graveside because of being a pallbearer, and because of his advanced age.

It was soon discovered that the casket wouldn't fit in the grave. Then it was discovered that those who had dug the grave had severed a water pipe and that it was slowly filling up with water. A number of men talked about this and then from the back of a pickup truck a generator and a water pump appeared. Three hundred people waited in steady rain for the pump to finish working and then watched while several men widened the grave so that the cedar casket could fit inside. When it was finally lowered a long line of men took turns shovelling dirt. This was accomplished quickly and soon the mound of earth was covered with wreaths and cedar boughs.

My friend worried about the severed pipe. Because the pipe had not been repaired when the water had been pumped out, he imagined the grave filling with water over the course of the following days and the casket slowly rising. But there was nothing he could do or say about this other than remark to the mourner beside him that they should put a note on the grave that said, *Don't worry, Sandy. It's just a high tide.*

The mourner gave a quiet laugh.

Around them other graves were decorated with plaster swans and lambs, faded plastic flowers, and spirit catchers, one made from a red hula hoop. Off to the side a hearse was parked and a white man in a black suit and with thin black hair stood beneath an umbrella. This was the funeral director who was also the owner and sole employee of C.A.R.E. Funeral Home.

Later there was a reception at the community hall. My friend was asked to read something he'd written about the chief. He said there was no formal introduction. Everyone was seated at long tables drinking pop. He followed an elder into the centre of the hall and the elder said, "This man is going to talk to you."

He began speaking and told people that it was unusual for a white man to address a group of Indians at a funeral. He then said he'd been asked to read something about the chief that he'd written for the local paper a few years ago. It was an article about the chief being a fisherman, and all the good he'd done for the community. He also told how the chief at the age of seventy-seven had raised his abandoned grandson, a fetal alcohol child who was now working on a prawn boat; thanks to the chief the boy was a good kid and had stayed away from dope and booze.

He then began reading the article. At first no one paid attention. There was no microphone and my friend is not a loud speaker. But he kept reading. Before long the hall became quiet. Everyone was listening. When he was through several people congratulated him and asked for a copy of the article. The schoolteacher was dispatched to make three hundred copies at the Indian school next door. Then everyone sat down to a baked ham dinner, even the funeral director, who was given the meal in consideration of his patience over the water-filled grave.

# WORKSHOP

I took a writing workshop from the guy who pumps gas at the local station. Doug. We met in the garage after hours and settled around a table that was placed next to the hoist that raises cars. A silver Toyota Corolla was suspended overhead like a mechanic's idea of a cloud.

There were three of us in the class. It really felt like a workshop with all those tools and workbenches, with slicks of grease and water on the floor.

Doug wore dirty coveralls

He had us do writing exercises. "I'll give each of you a random word," he said, and flung open a dictionary. "When you get your word you have fifteen minutes. Write something."

My word was "intimate." The woman next to me got "terror." Lucky her. She scribbled away. The young man at the end of the table got "shine." He exceeded all expectations and wrote a five-part service manual.

## OUR HERO

Mooly Banks, that woman over there in the white apron, is our hero. She's the one who climbs the cliff each morning to the very top. Climbs over craggy rock with her baby strapped to her chest. From down here we watch through binoculars as she picks her way over the mouths, noses, and foreheads of our ancestors, the men and women whose likenesses are carved into the cliff side. No one except Mooly Banks ever reaches the top, or even tries, because the top is miles up there. We know she's finally reached her destination when the sky starts to lower towards us. This is because Mooly Banks has grabbed the thick rope that dangles between the stars and is pulling and pulling on it. When she pulls the rope the cliff descends too, eventually to flatten out like squished clay. Soon enough we can look at the faces of our ancestors up close like they were intricately designed paving stones. Tracing our hands over their softened features gives us pleasure and is more intimate than gazing at them from afar.

# CHOKING MAN

At the restaurant a man at the next table was choking. Fortunately I knew St. John's Ambulance and though I'd never had a chance to practise it, I remembered a few things: how to make a sling, how to test for breathing, how to make a finger splint out of Popsicle sticks, how to perform the Heimlich Manoeuvre. So I leapt from my chair. I was excited; finally here was someone I could save. As expected the choking man looked like a choking man: red face, bulging eyes, hands clenching the throat. There was a woman sitting beside him, a fork poised at her mouth. She had grey hair and wore a ladybug broach. I presumed she was his wife. There was a look of speechless horror on her face, the same look I'd seen in science-fiction movies. I understood what the look described. It was the same speechless horror I'd experienced watching a documentary film at school when I was ten. Thanks to that film speechless horror became one of my stock reactions to life. If there is even a whiff of speechless horror in my vicinity—something read, something imagined or seen, something feared—I am there with a pounding heart. And the school documentary is the cause of this. It was done in black and white, in the style of *Psycho*. A family sits having dinner. It's an ordinary day, a Tuesday, say, nothing remarkable about it. The soundtrack music skips and tinkles. It's a happy scene, much like a scene from a *Dick and Jane* reader, that earlier world of sweet family life. Suddenly the music changes—screech, boom—and the daughter, who is the same age as those in the audience, starts choking and falls to the floor. Her parents leap from the table. Now the soundtrack is frenzied, out-of-tune violins. The mother screams and wrings her apron; the father kneels by the girl and looks frantic; the little brother, in his striped T-shirt and buzz cut, runs around in circles, demented. It's clear, nobody knows what to do. The girl writhes on the floor. The music builds, grating, urgent. Then the father jumps up and grabs the carving knife from the table. Moments before it was carving the family roast. Now we know it will be used to hack open the girl's throat so she can breathe. The fright of the audience is acute. We are a roomful of children speechless with horror. Some of us are crying. I will have nightmares about this scene for years to come. Even though in an instant the film cuts to a doctor's office and a man in a lab coat says that such a tragedy need never occur. His voice is soothing. He may have said, "Now, children, you wouldn't want this to happen to your friends Susie or Billy, would you?" He says it's up to us. We can save people. All we have to do is learn first aid. The film then returns to the panicked family. Now, instead of grabbing the carving knife, the father grabs his daughter from behind and pulls her to a half-standing position. We then witness the Heimlich Manoeuvre. A second later the piece of meat is in the mother's hands and everyone is hugging. Once again the music skips and tinkles. I remembered all of this at the restaurant. I moved towards the choking man with urgency. I really wanted to save him. Gripping him from behind, I gave a mighty pull on his chest. It didn't take long. A wad of chewed steak shot to the floor. The man gasped. Then panted, and wiped his face with his hand. I've heard this said of rescuers: they think of nothing else but the rescue at hand. Some say it's like having an out-of-body experience— the single-minded drive, the complete absence of thought for one's self. This is certainly true. It is a state I would like to experience on a full-time basis. Because of this I am always on the lookout for a choking man. In fact, I am thinking of organizing a Choking Man Festival. It would be held every summer in the interior of British Columbia. A week would be devoted to the many creative ways in which we can rescue one another from speechless horror. There would be practical demonstrations and strange ceremonies, position papers and impromptu debates. There would be music, dancing, drug taking, laughing—much laughing. The banners would be ironic and read: *Did You Mean for Me to Scream?* On the final night a two-hundred-foot-tall choking man would be mounted above the festival goers. Then at midnight, amidst cheering and horn blowing, fireworks would shoot from the choking man's mouth.

## INSIDE THE BUS STATION

There was a slaughterhouse inside the bus station. Waiting for my bus I watched a group of children playing tag amongst the hung carcasses, running with meat cleavers in their hands, slipping in the blood, and laughing. When a small girl flung a chicken at a boy's head, knocking him to the ground, I rushed over. "Go play somewhere else," I yelled. Eighty-five chickens a minute were having their throats slashed by a mechanical arm, each chicken hanging from hooks that whizzed past the seated people waiting for the bus. "Go find something else to do," I told the children, the line of chickens forming a bloody curtain that obscured the splendid cityscape the bus would soon take us through ...

## TO THE LEFT OF REASON

For many years she's been wearing a special key around her neck like a locket, a key given to her by her father before he died. And she's just realized that the key unlocks a certain door in the night—one located somewhere to the left of reason. And it's because of this key that she can take a vacation, can vacate her usual life for a period of time. And it gets even better because while she enjoys her escape, the dead will be banished to the wings like stand-ins at a vaudeville show and won't be allowed to join meals or hog conversation or offer up aphorisms the way they usually do. They'll be rendered mute and immobile and *their* special keys, the ones dangling from their waists on thick chains, will be revealed as the vulgar accessory they really are.

## BIRDS OF PREY, THEIR HEADS BOWED ...

Some are displayed in shop windows, stuffed and mounted, their glass eyes staring downwards. Some perch in tall firs and bow to impotence as others, numerous as driftwood, wash up along the shore. Still others hold quiet services on city rooftops. Murmuring, they ask one another, What to do? What to do?

# WORLD'S LONGEST PROTEST MARCH

Fifty-five hundred years and counting ...

## WORLD'S LONGEST PROTEST MARCH—
## SECOND PLACE

A thirty-eight-year march down First Street. With placards, bullhorns, and shifts spelling each other off at four-hour intervals. An umbrella organization, a collaboration of complaints, a melting pot, a dumping ground for public worry. The protest of *everything*—including squandered natural resources, tainted personalities, predator corporations, the shoddy treatment of anything, anything attached to the word "lack." Nothing is exempt. Anyone can join as long as they pay the fees, fulfill the sign regulations. Loggers march alongside eco-terrorists; babies with placards attached to their buggies protest plastic diapers; pensioners protest death. Etcetera. At the end of each shift, every protester is guaranteed an audience at the pavilion—even if the audience is with each other.

The town where the protest occurs has become famous. A sign at the town's entrance says, *Home of the World's Longest Protest March!* The attendant benefits are in place. Tour busses, TV shows. Etcetera.

## WORLD'S LONGEST PROTEST MARCH—
## HONOURABLE MENTION

Protestantism—excluding interruptions ...

# THREE DUD PETS

A man buys his girlfriend a tarantula. When it crawls up her bare arm she says it feels like sandpaper. She says, It's kinda cute, but is it fixed?

Oh, no, says the man, it's still poisonous. Don't make any sudden moves.

The girlfriend must now baby-step around the house.

Next the man gets her a rat that weighs seven pounds and has oversized yellow teeth. Some kind of mutant, says the man.

The rat drapes itself around the girlfriend's neck and won't be moved. I dunno, says the girlfriend, what if it bites?

Don't worry, says the man, just don't get it mad.

The girlfriend must now keep her head bowed due to the weight of the rat and wear a plastic shawl to protect her clothing.

Finally the man gets her a scabby grey cat that has a bowel problem and shits on the girlfriend's shoes.

That's it! cries the girlfriend. The cat's the sign I've been waiting for! Because when a man gives his girlfriend three dud pets in a row it means the wedding is off!

She throws the rat from her neck and bolts out the door.

Thwarted, the man takes the tarantula, the rat, and the cat for a long walk off a short pier.

He thinks this is the end of the story but he's wrong. Because death has transformed the three dud pets into stars of a cartoon movie. United by hate and revenge they embark on a journey. Their mission? To find the man and scratch, bite, poison, and shit on him until he's dead.

Along the way they have adventures. The world is a huge litter box for the cat; the rat and the tarantula terrify many small children. The three become close friends—when the tarantula gets tired it jumps on the rat's back; the cat's bowel problem is discreetly ignored.

Passing through a city one night a shoe gets thrown at the tarantula and it loses two legs. This is when the tarantula's fine tenor voice is revealed. It breaks into song ... beneath the lonely street light ... while the cat and the rat struggle to re-attach its legs ...

.Later, in a clear-cut, the trio meets up with a colony of sympathetic red ants who guide them to the highway. There they find the man's car parked by the side of the road. He's passed out on the back seat.

Drunk again, says the rat.

We can wait, says the cat.

*Ave Maria*, sings the tarantula.

It's mid-day when the man wakes up to find them perched on his chest. He screams and screams, but it's no use ...

Afterwards, at a gas station, an attendant chases the rat with a broom and accidentally severs a gas main. Somehow a lit match gets thrown into the mix and the place explodes spectacularly.

Only the dud pets survive.

They head off beneath a shower of sparks. Beyond—a full yellow moon, an empty road.

Maybe they'll find the girlfriend and move in with her, maybe not ...

## IN REVERSE

The idea that the Earth is hollow gained attention in 1946 when Rodney Shaver, a writer and scientist, reported visiting an underground city for several weeks and living there with demons that were talented, brilliant, and urbane. Hideous-looking, too, but Rodney Shaver could allow for that because the demons were so cultured. It wasn't safe up top, they said, with the wars and atrocities. So they fled underground.

Civilization—you can have it!

Rodney Shaver described the inside of Earth as a vast living room filled with couches and chandeliers. There, demons wearing silk dressing gowns practised transcendence in reverse. Herman Hesse came in for a lot of *bon mots*.

Fifty years later and it's still not safe up top. Most of the demons still don't want anything to do with humans. But rumour has it they're running out of champagne and *bon mots*.

# PASSION

His passion is collecting pennies. These he places lovingly over the eyes of dead field mice ...

Her passion is starring the imagination, catching rides on paper planes ...

Sometimes they are passionate together and practise random Buddhism—we'll notice this ... and this ...

They are grateful for the shelter their passions bring. Life can be a closet paradise, they say, as long as we keep our passions ...

# DIVINATION—THE THORNY PRACTICE OF WANTS

1. If you want to sweat with inspiration then have your picture taken in the VIP lounge of any major airport because there you'll find the most powerful and famous men and women in all the gilded kingdom who will kiss you for a price and most often for free and in kissing them you will discover that they are really simple-minded people and lonely for the sort of gripping conversation that only you can provide because their usual utterances are limited to exclamations like *My these elevator floors are slippery!* and further that they have nothing in their wallets but pictures of themselves and even if you travelled with them down a fifty-mile elevator they'd still be showing you the pictures and you would be duly inspired.

2. If you want to be invited to the wedding the parade and all the parties then first travel with a band of Gypsies across Europe like revolutionaries marching to the capital with banners and patriotic songs and then assist them with the buying (or stealing) of new luggage from a large department store and be sure to help whenever you can without being asked.

3. If you want to feed the world's starving then first you have to work at a concession stand at the Winter Olympics because only there instead of ringing up bags of hamburgers and fries and submarine sandwiches for grandmothers in fur coats treating the family to a takeout meal will you discover the true program that will send food by fax to those most in need and further you will discover the program that converts pictures

of fat hams into real hams at the other end and you'll press the start button and food will crash through computer screens all over the world and to the starving this will be like winning at the slot machines in Las Vegas.

4. If you want to join that select group called Doctors Without Conscience which is a movement and a recreation dedicated to the execution of criminals engaged in the seediest kinds of activities—drug dealers, stolen electronics salesmen, pimps—and which invariably ends in the stealthy pharmaceutical murder of said criminals by Doctors Without Conscience so that the killing is handled like some biological principle like some imperative to rid the world of vermin then make sure you have the necessary prerequisites namely the ability to finance costly vacations to Mexico or the Bahamas and to enroll your children in private schools and also to own several residences and employ bodyguards.

5. If you want to be a good companion giving all you can the bright view in spite of everything the crying laughter and so on then you must write a book of poems whereby your heart is arranged carefully on each page so that it becomes a little feast for anyone to nibble on.

# PERPETUAL CODA

## I.

We bring our perfect intelligence to bear upon the situation, which is to say, our lives, which is to say our reasons; where the essential story is the one in which the world outlives our dreams, where human death outlives our knowing; where the sorry view is the one in which we stand, step, weep, and die; where bitterness produces stories that caricature mankind, hence our need for love, that neutralizing force we wear on our sleeves like an IV drip of soda; where memory is the salvation of the retired and the overwhelmed, but frequently a gift we give ourselves; where most understandings are accidental, the result of an ontological crapshoot; where self-admiration is a violent knowing that obscures all light; where the mythical forest is ourselves; where we lunch on lyric expressions, imagining rescue, escape; where our time demands simplicity as counterpoint to excessive detail—or so it seems—like a basic formula; where I am a woman stumbling without hope towards enlightenment as surely as if it were heaven; where I am a woman whose steps are dogged by violent reasons.

## 2.

We bring our perfect intelligence to bear upon uncertain
metaphysical points; where hope propels us towards heart-
breaking wisdoms; where any church attempts to neutralize
the natural acids that would caricature mankind; where love
is our reward delivered often without enlightenment as
though through a fog; where we lunch on various Buddhas
still imagining rescue, escape; where hope is pinned on eter-
nity; where thinking demands simplicity as counterpoint to
excessive heart; where I am a woman participating in the
small-time greedy view; where I am a woman stumbling
towards love, light, and the mythical forest.

## 3.

We bring our hunger to bear upon the situation, which is to say, our reasons; where the story, like a basic dream, is the one in which we stand, step, weep, and die; where understanding is frequently accidental, or the result of formula; where some of us engage in the work of archiving metaphors; where some of us can name at least seven bitter stories that caricature mankind; where love is the story of our heartbreaking wisdoms; where memory is the story of our IV drip of routine, which is to say, our violent knowing; where in every human death there is a story about land mines; where I am a woman stumbling towards the perpetual coda; where I am a woman stumbling as though through a fog.

# 5.

# The Breakdown So Far

# BREAKDOWN OF THE MONTH CALENDAR

**January.** Outside, the everlasting wheezes and falters. The dog poses on the community picnic table then vanishes. The town is flabby and grey. At home there is a tight limit on table language.

**February.** Mother's mind goes missing on a drive for soft ice-cream. A return to the picnic table turns up a bird's skull. Grandma wears work boots and lime-green stretch pants to Grandpa's funeral. The language on the fridge magnet says *You Are Loved*.

**March.** At home Mother's mind is found buried beneath the laundry. Sister writes a poem in praise of emotion. A new dog is bought and named Odysseus. Outside, the everlasting is crackling and green.

**April.** It rains on the town for thirty straight days. For thirty days Brother watches TV. Father unplugs the sink, the toilet, and the storm drains. Mother's mind scurries off in a torrent of ditch water.

**May.** Brother gets a prize for taking a bath. Grandma wears a black sarong and bare feet to Old Age Bingo. Sister writes a hymn about dread. The planet tilts nearer the sun.

**June.** Outside, the everlasting bubbles and bursts. Mother's mind returns inside a yellow helium balloon. The balloon settles in a back-yard tree and glows at night like a lamp. Father lies on the living room rug laughing hysterically.

**July.** Odysseus begins his wanderings through the blue and silver town. The balloon bursts when a robin lands on its surface. Grandma breaks her arm climbing the tree to gather pieces of Mother's mind. The robin is taken to the vet.

**August.** The car breaks down on a trip for Krazy Glue. For two weeks, the glue keeps Mother's mind attached to her brain. One evening the everlasting, the town, and Mother's mind are cast in a lovely bronze light. The car breaks down on a trip for pizza.

**September.** Brother wins a prize for taking out the garbage. Mother gets a new broom to commemorate renewed effort. Grandma gets a new pot to bang on because she's not dead yet. Brother wins new love—the vet's comely assistant.

**October.** Mother's mind hitches a ride on her broom and soars towards the moon. Father says the trick in life is to keep your eyes averted. Grandma says the treat is hardly worth the effort. Grandma runs off with the bingo caller.

**November.** Outside, the everlasting is ragged and brown. Odysseus returns with Mother's mind on a leash. Father lies on the kitchen floor laughing and laughing. The planet tilts away from the sun.

**December.** Sister writes a poem about renewal. Brother wins a prize for leaving home. Mother's mind is housed with the budgie. The car breaks down on a trip for birdseed.

## LARGE MOMENTS

A family is having a conversation about large moments.

I've had it with those bloated over-achievers, says the father. All they do is make you tremble. What's the point?

Exactly, says the mother. Plus they're too big to swallow. I'm always gagging on mine.

They make me faint, says their daughter. Who can take in everything at once?

If you want my opinion, they're exhausting, says the son-in-law. Especially when they won't stop coming. Like—Oh great, another large moment. They wear me out.

I'd rather sleep or eat potatoes or read the newspaper or clean a pot than have a large moment, says the mother.

Having a large moment sounds like having a dump, says the daughter.

Yeah, says the son-in-law. What's so amazing about that?

Whose dumb idea was large moments anyway? asks the grandpa. Aren't small moments bad enough? Why expand on things?

You've got that right, says the father. I've had it with sudden wilderness frights ... with being seized by revelations ...

Some idiot, says the daughter, wrote a book that said you'd get more bang for your buck if you lived your life having large moments. Get a load of this: *A large moment is an opening in the stretch of time.*

Sounds like having a tumor, says the son-in-law.

As far as I'm concerned, says the grandpa, large moments can take a hike. They're bewildering. And you know where bewilderment leads.

Too true, says the father. Remember? *Bewilderment is the attitude of the human being seized by desperation in the shipwreck of existence.*

There you go, says the grandpa.

It's small moments that keep the ship afloat, says the mother.

That, and the scientific method, says the daughter.

We're animals. We need our mindless rest ...

It's species survival ...

We need to shut down and recoup ...

Think of the baby, says the mother. The baby needs protecting.

So it's agreed, says the father. From now on there'll be no more large moments. Our lives will be Large Moment Free Zones.

Safety, at last, says the mother.

What a relief, says the grandpa. I've had more large moments than I'd care to mention.

Oh, oh, says the son-in-law. Look out the window. There's a large moment heading towards the house.

What does it want? cries the daughter.

The usual, says the mother. Wonder. Terror. Divine interruption.

It looks like a tornado, cries the daughter.

Don't panic, cries the father.

Down to the cellar, cries the grandpa.

Get a grip, says the mother. And would somebody please cover the baby's eyes before it's too late?

# THE BREAKDOWN SO FAR

*On the Subject of Literature*

## I.

Wondered if the vision was worthwhile or if it was dumb; a gully; an antique. Wondered if there was too much feeling about everything, too much seeing of the world's despair. Was over-full with thinking about the tragicomic; the impotence to help or change; the indulgence of seeking perfectly executed moments of attention and regard; the dabbling in nuclear thought, the fabulously impossible, the impossibly rubbishy, the next uncertainty, the next fresh wind. Wondered about the necessity of gratification tricks, the increased wattage of personal pleasure to maintain, if not blindness, then the covert, sidelong view. Could not shut up for wondering.

## 2.

Referred to our former quirky nurses, the surrealists, the cubists, the beats; observed them acting like volunteer workers for the blind; suggesting the story; the validity of the inspired haul; suffering, and all the rest; tigers, even; the slow shining of expanded connections; the particular voice—thunder! And the absurd; strangeness; the laughter at our scary salesmanship, our arbitrary watchwords—silence; visuals; the scientific method; words; exile; your brother in Disneyland; cunning; song. Remembered: it's a long walk to find a new mind. Remembered: "No new line without a new mind."

## 3.

Wondered if it is tragicomic that the times we are having now appear on TV in rapid collage, sometimes animated; that our authenticity, as a result, is frequently robbed; that the speed of duplication between what we are and how we are presented further erases reflection, distance, and history; that we are forever here in the lukewarm soup; that there is a living paradise but it's looking dour; that Blake is standing at a low window mourning, not the craft, but the content; that Lorca is fondling his rosary of deaths like an obsessive-compulsive; that irony is eroding fast, like sandstone; that the Dadaists continue to go mad; that, both fearing and yearning for anonymity, many now abandon their art with a grunt.

# 4.

Assembled the mental health equipment: arrested hopelessness; understood the short rules of meditation and deconstruction; kept skepticism intact; removed self-indulgence; maintained connection to the universe; maintained manoeuvrability; stood witness. Understood the risks: reducing experience to a focus, a narrative arc, the solipsistic, the short light story; suspending thoughts and minds; sweeping aside the large, the inanimate world; regarding dreams as unworthy; exalting over never lived-in days; nominating oneself for results, for masterpieces; allowing the quest for celebrity to overtake and becoming lost, eaten; keeping Buddha like some high-end perceptual pet.

## 5.

Admired Norman Levine and Peter Handke, wandering about on trains, and in cities, looking out windows; noting details; the outside world revealed precisely—small events closely observed: snow melting; a parade of hats at a train station; a butterfly's wobble; glow worms; a red-tailed hawk flying across a field of snow. Working at their desks in some high room, alone in winter; draughts through the window frame; a storm brewing, sheet lightning. A kind of exaltation prose, but precise, not hysterical like hunger; prose that tends the fire and the shop; about the fascination with things; in living errant; in randomness and beautiful days; the distinctive now, including moments of sourness; imagination; record keeping; great dread; wild laughs, trembling sweeps; the eye trained for memory; understanding the face of horror but letting the saint be large. Remembered that Chekhov is behind this notion.

# 6.

Described the irrelevant. Trained the humour. Removed blinkers. Kept the furnishings spare. Feared history. Shunned electronic truths. Shunned money. Remembered that the history of love has resulted in one melody. Traipsed after some Chinese man's sayings, some Indian's, some woman's. Traipsed after an audience. Celebrated both the nightmare and the delight. Trapped experience with words. Exploded, on occasion, with pandemonium. Attempted to melt self-consciousness. Canvassed door to door with song. Scythed moribund visions. Memorized the times. Specified edginess. Maintained aspects of the idiot, the faithful brain. Caught the train. Missed the train. Was found guilty. Was found innocent.

# 7.

Considered the ideas we funnel into art: the sexual ones; the
lives of resurgence; absence; playfulness; merriment; weird
fantasy; fakes; fresh views merrily running; making reckless
irony enlightenment, a spectacle of encounter; making it
very shiny; filling it with heart; spending the world; making
melodies of essential truths; creating symphonies, Czeslaws
of wonder, everyone with a measure of delight, everyone
capable of levitation; remembering former artists and the
singular stroke, O'Keefe, for one, and the sublimity of her
vision; remembering the lovely black recourse of Burroughs
and the days spent in cafés bemoaning the brass conscious-
ness of others; remembering Nabokov's grim monster of
common sense and how it must be shot dead; constructing a
mental aerobics with stories that include love and the slap of
explanation; that include nerve, unadorned; finding what
excites, finally, like something pure ...

# ACKNOWLEDGEMENTS

The author thanks the Canada Council for the Arts for its generous support.

Grateful thanks also to the editors of the publications/places where sections of the book first appeared: *Fiddlehead Magazine*, 2005 and CBC Radio I, broadcast in 2004, "Now is the Time"; *The Vancouver Sun*, 2006, "The Compassionate Side of Nature" (as "Dachshund in Danger Where Eagles Soar"); *This Magazine*, 2005, "Because of Russell Edson"; *This Magazine*, 2005, "Sixty Degrees," which was also a finalist in the 2006 National Magazine Awards for Fiction; *71 for GB*, an anthology for George Bowering, 2006, Coach House Press, edited by Jean Baird, requested piece, "Happy Birthday"; *radiant danse uv being, a poetic portrait of bill bissett*, Nightwood Editions, 2006, requested piece, "A Universe Runs Through Him"; *Geist Magazine*, 2006, "Budgie Suicide," "Funeral," "Hens"; *The Women's Post*, Toronto, 2004 and CBC Radio I, broadcast in 2004, "Fine, Thank You"; Alma Lee Tribute, 2006, requested piece, "A Day so Happy"; *Fiddlehead Magazine*, 2005, "Divination— The Thorny Practice of Wants"; *Adbusters Magazine*, 2005, Art Fart Issue, "The Breakdown So Far."

\* \* \*

Quotes used: "Valentine"—Samuel Beckett; "Inseparably Linked"— P. T. Barnum; "Tour"—Russell Edson, Arno Holz, R. Crumb; "Shift Work"—W. C. Fields; "Bad Boy"—Kurt Vonnegut; "A Universe Runs Through Him"—Jane Eaton Hamilton, Russell Edson; "Choking Man"—Mike Myers; "Large Moments"—Cornelis Verhoeven; "The Breakdown so Far," #2—William Carlos Williams.